10 Things to Do Before the Apocalypse

When happily married Jake and Santino head to the bars on Seattle's Capitol Hill to pick up a third for the night, they don't realize they're about to hook up with a dead man.

Only they can see and interact with Andy, stabbed to death near Pioneer Square a few days earlier. Finally convinced that Andy really has been murdered, Jake and Santino join forces with his ghost to track down the killer.

Did Andy's jealous ex do it? His spurned coworker? A right-wing vigilante?

As the trio investigates, police and coworkers begin to suspect Jake and Santino may be mentally ill…or the murderers themselves.

Will they be arrested? Institutionalized?

Amidst escalating political tensions, Jake and Santino begin to fall in love with Andy. But what will become of him when the killer is found?

And what happens if the killer comes after Jake and Santino next?

Praise for Johnny Townsend

In *Zombies for Jesus*, "Townsend isn't writing satire, but deeply emotional and revealing portraits of people who are, with a few exceptions, quite lovable."

        Kel Munger, *Sacramento News and Review*

In *Sex among the Saints,* "Townsend writes with a deadpan wit and a supple, realistic prose that's full of psychological empathy....he takes his protagonists' moral struggles seriously and invests them with real emotional resonance."

        Kirkus Reviews

Inferno in the French Quarter: The UpStairs Lounge Fire is "a gripping account of all the horrors that transpired that night, as well as a respectful remembrance of the victims."

        Terry Firma, Patheos

"Johnny Townsend's 'Partying with St. Roch' [in the anthology *Latter-Gay Saints*] tells a beautiful, haunting tale."

        Kent Brintnall, Out in Print: Queer Book Reviews

Selling the City of Enoch is "sharply intelligent...pleasingly complex...The stories are full of...doubters, but there's no vindictiveness in these pages; the characters continuously poke holes in Mormonism's more extravagant absurdities, but they take very little pleasure in doing so....Many of Townsend's stories...have a provocative edge to them, but this [book] displays a great deal of insight as well...a playful, biting and surprisingly warm collection."

Kirkus Reviews

Gayrabian Nights is "an allegorical tour de force...a hard-core emotional punch."

Gay. Guy. Reading and Friends

The Washing of Brains has "A lovely writing style, and each story [is] full of unique, engaging characters....immensely entertaining."

Rainbow Awards

In *Dead Mankind Walking*, "Townsend writes in an energetic prose that balances crankiness and humor....A rambunctious volume of short, well-crafted essays..."

Kirkus Reviews

10 Things to Do Before the Apocalypse

Johnny Townsend

Johnny Townsend

Copyright © 2024 Johnny Townsend

Print ISBN: 978-1-961525-20-7
Ebook ISBN: 978-1-961525-23-8

All rights reserved. No part of this publication may be reproduced, stored in a retrieval system, or transmitted in any form or by any means, electronic, mechanical, recording, or otherwise, without the prior written permission of the author.

This book is a work of fiction. Names, characters, events, and dialogue are the product of the author's imagination or are used fictitiously. Any resemblance to actual persons, living or dead, is entirely coincidental.

Printed on acid-free paper.

2024

First Edition

Cover design by Blazing Covers

Contents

Chapter One: Santino 9

Chapter Two: Jake 20

Chapter Three: Andy 31

Chapter Four: Santino 40

Chapter Five: Jake 53

Chapter Six: Andy 65

Chapter Seven: Santino 78

Chapter Eight: Santino 86

Chapter Nine: Jake 93

Chapter Ten: Andy 105

Chapter Eleven: Santino 114

Chapter Twelve: Santino 124

Chapter Thirteen: Jake 135

Chapter Fourteen: Andy 148

Chapter Fifteen: Andy 154

Chapter Sixteen: Santino 164

Chapter Seventeen: Jake 174

Chapter Eighteen: Jake 185

Epilogue: Andy 192

Books by Johnny Townsend 197
What Readers Have Said 207

Chapter One: Santino

I only took two psychology courses in college—Psych 101 and Adolescent Psychology—but the course I *should* have taken was Abnormal Psychology. Without it, I found myself looking online now for answers.

And not finding anything that didn't sound like a conspiracy theory.

How could my husband Jake and I both experience the exact same hallucination? Were the worsening conflicts in the Middle East, the far right gaining ground in Europe, and growing fascism in the U.S. enough to create so much anxiety that we both dissociated from reality at the same instant?

Was it the mushrooms I bought from a coworker, hoping to alleviate a minor bout of depression from discovering *Brooklyn Nine Nine* only after Andre Braugher had already died?

I suppose I should start at the moment of our psychotic break, if you can trust the account of a mentally unstable man. I'm writing all this down as accurately as I can remember for future researchers. Perhaps we'll be a footnote in someone's dissertation one day.

Fifteen seconds of fame.

"Hey, Santino," said Jake, rubbing my back while I washed dishes in the sink, "you up for a night out?"

"Depends." I rinsed soap off the last bowl and set it in the dishrack. "Who are you in the mood for?"

Jake and I had been a couple for twenty-three years, married for twelve. Neither of us had ever wanted monogamy but also found we enjoyed each other so much that we rarely played outside the relationship. In the beginning, we'd play separately every few months and then, over the years, we learned we preferred playing together, a bit more since the pandemic eased up. We were both versatile, after all. We liked the same activities (pretty much anything that didn't involve pain). And we liked the same physical type—guys who looked and dressed the way we did. Dad bods. Well, grandad bods these days. And beards.

We had matching T-shirts reading "Narcissists R Us."

Jake and I liked almost anyone with dark hair and furry chests. We typically wore black jeans and T-shirts. Polos if we were feeling fancy. Technically bears, neither Jake nor I was excessively heavy, though we could both stand to lose twenty or thirty pounds. And while we were especially attracted to guys our age and weight, we'd had sex with guys as young as thirty and as old as eighty, with slim guys as well as men who weighed close to three hundred.

We had a type, but we weren't married to it.

Well, except for the one marriage.

"I'm in the mood for a two-hour session with a guy who will stay the night."

"Glad I took a nap before dinner."

"I added extra protein powder in the salsa."

"That's not the way I prefer to get my extra protein."

"Which is why we're going out," Jake said. "It's Friday. Buddies will be the best place to scout."

On Seattle's Capitol Hill, Buddies was just down the block from the new five-story gay senior living apartments. Over the years, our dark hair had morphed into salt and pepper, but in our heads, salt and pepper still translated into brunet.

Of course, we were the only two men we knew who used that term.

"Sounds good. A Buddies bear it is."

Perhaps it wasn't the generalized political anxiety that caused what happened next. It may not even have been the mushrooms a few days earlier. Besides an occasional brownie, neither of us voluntarily used other drugs, but we were about to be introduced to something new.

We caught light rail near our home in Rainier Beach. The ride proceeded smoothly until the train stopped between stations in the Beacon Hill tunnel, the lights blinking out. As we waited five minutes, then ten, for power to come back on, someone lit up and began puffing.

Weed, sure, but there was a note of something else, too.

Body odor? Or…?

I'd just started groping Jake to make better use of our time when the lights flashed back on and the train continued toward downtown.

"Prick tease," he whispered when I withdrew my hand.

"Ass tease," I whispered back.

"Mouth tease."

"Nipple tease."

An Asian man across the aisle cleared his throat. Jake patted my thigh. I nudged his knee.

Fifteen minutes later, we emerged from the light rail station on Broadway. Seattle's gay neighborhood had changed enormously over the past three decades. Still marginally gay, it was far more gentrified, with dozens of tall, new apartment buildings and condos, home to growing numbers of tech workers.

It was also crammed with dozens, perhaps hundreds, of homeless folks living in the parks, along the freeway, in alleys, in their cars, wherever they could find a spot. Last month, someone took a baseball bat and killed a homeless man while he slept. Just a few days ago, someone deliberately drove an SUV onto the sidewalk to mow down three tents, killing a homeless woman.

The driver got away.

Jake and I passed a gay bar a white supremacist had tried to set on fire a few years before.

Did I mention we were feeling anxious?

When we reached Buddies, the bouncer checked our IDs. "I'll find an empty spot," Jake told me. "Could you get us some beer?"

"What's the magic word?"

"Hangover?" Jake suggested. "Beer enema? Sloppy kisses?"

"You never were very good at math."

"Threesome?"

I wagged a finger in his face. "The magic word is always blowjob."

"The magic word is *crass*?" Jake wrinkled his nose.

"No, it's blowjob."

"Who's on first?"

"Who cums first?"

"What were we talking about?"

The bar scene had also changed a good deal since Jake and I both came out in the 1980s, in ways that often felt disconcerting. Of course, back in the day, we had the anxiety of knowing a single wrong move could get us infected with a deadly, incurable virus. Why we didn't have our psychotic break back then, I don't know.

Perhaps we were developing synchronized dementia in our early sixties?

I liked to point out that Jake was eight months older than me.

Jake liked to point out he had more life experience than I did and so his vote counted more when we had difficult decisions to make. Like what color to paint the porch chairs.

He insisted on eggplant purple, and I have to admit, he was right.

Despite the proximity of the senior living apartments, the crowd tonight looked exceptionally young. Men mostly in their thirties. I'd felt mature when I was their age. Like an adult. Responsible.

I tried not to think about all the things these young men didn't know. Such as life before cell phones and computers and streaming. Before Uber and Grindr and TikTok.

Before PrEP.

Things were not great now. But they weren't any better then.

At least now, Jake and I could watch Belgian shows like *Beau Sejour*, Brazilian shows like *Nobody's Looking*. American shows like *Sense8*, which would never grow old.

I bought two beers and handed one to Jake, sidling up next to him to better survey the crowd.

"Everybody's already with friends," Jake commented. "No one's free to join us."

"Try to catch someone's eye," I said. "Give them a come hither look."

"Like Lucy Ricardo in the Great Train Robbery?"

"Like Mae West in *I'm No Angel*."

Jake snorted. "I can match the drawl, but I'm not sure there's enough light for anyone to see my come hither look."

"We could turn on our cell phone flashlights," I suggested. "Wave them in the air and sing 'Want to Want Me.'"

"Your mouth is three inches from my ear, Santino. And I can barely hear *you*."

Jake's banter was beginning to feel less banterish and more curmudgeony. This seemed to be happening more often lately, though usually later in the evening, not this early in our quest. We were good looking "for our age," but fewer and fewer men were interested in guys our age. We'd tried the various hookup sites and found that men liked to *say* they were interested and yet somehow rarely found the time to finally meet. No one liked sexual rejection, even if you weren't going home alone. These sexual adventures had begun feeling too much like long waits in Urgent Care.

It was almost enough to make a couple monogamous.

Over the next forty-five minutes, Jake and I did what we could to attract the attention of men walking by. We kissed each other. We discussed gay celebrity gossip. We tweaked each other's nipples. We talked about an article I'd read earlier that day boasting "4 Reasons Humans Will Beat Climate Change."

"The first reason was, 'Humans are smart.'"

"In other words, we're fucked."

I sighed and surveyed the crowd again. "I'm keeping my fingers crossed," I said. "Toes, too."

"Arthritis doesn't count."

We groped each other and kissed again. Still no interest. I figured we should probably just go ahead and have a real conversation. It was far too easy to let the days pass without talking about anything meaningful. Especially since serious topics were so damn serious.

Was it technically "quality time" if the meaningful discussion was dreary?

"Republicans introduced a bill in some red state to have Animal Services remove children in school who identify as furries," I said.

"Trump's selling pieces of his suit jacket like religious relics," Jake replied.

"A power plant was bombed in Ukraine."

"They caught someone running over sex workers on Aurora," Jake said.

"The Washington State GOP made opposing democracy an official part of their platform."

Did I mention that *everyone* was under a great deal of psychological stress these days?

"Should we just head to the baths, Santino, and put our legs into some stirrups?" Jake rubbed the back of his head, always a sign he was feeling anxious. I'd warned him he'd go bald if he kept it up, but so far, he still had a full head of hair.

And me? I'd rather not talk about it.

I looked around the bar once more. Lots of young men laughing and drinking and probably not even aware of our existence.

There comes a point in every aging gay man's life when he needs to accept reality.

I kissed Jake on his furry cheek. "Let's get out of here."

We hadn't taken two steps, though, before a young man in his early forties climbed onto a table halfway across the room and started shouting. "Pay attention to me!" Even from this distance, I could see that at least one button on his black jeans was undone. He waved about like a right-wing school board member swatting at a kaleidoscope of trans butterflies.

Not exactly sexy behavior. But his slight paunch looked inviting as it stretched his red T-shirt. Jake and I looked at one another and shrugged before turning back to the man on the table. I started a slow clap and Jake joined in. "Why didn't *we* think of that?" I asked.

"Well, I did suggest the stirrups," Jake reminded me. "It's pretty much the same thing."

No one else seemed to appreciate the young man's strategy, ignoring him rather coldly. Gay etiquette left a lot to be desired. I tried to make myself stop thinking of the butterfly swatter as young, which wasn't easy. It was unfair, though, a way of diminishing him. And made me feel way too old.

Jake and I maneuvered our way to the man's table. Two men in their early thirties saw us approach and moved away. I looked up at the guy. He was our type, dark haired, with a beard that perhaps wasn't as trim as I preferred, maybe half an inch long, something that would feel good against my ass. Like us, he was probably twenty pounds above what was considered optimal in judgmental society.

I reached up and offered my hand. "Inexpensive advertising," I said, "but effective. We'd join you up there, but I don't think the table could handle it."

The man's mouth fell open.

"You're too young to feel so invisible," Jake commiserated. "We don't want to say, 'Wait until you're *our* age,' but…"

"Want to come home with us?" I asked.

"Yes!"

Excellent, I thought. No games. No playing hard to get. We were all here for the same reason. No sense pretending.

The man quickly climbed down from the table. He hugged us both with far too much desperation, and I began second guessing myself. Horny was one thing, but no one liked a clingy, needy man. Jake and I exchanged a nervous glance.

Then the man kissed me, his tongue large and thick, filling my mouth, and tasting slightly of ginger. Despite his earlier frantic state, he now seemed to relax into the kiss. I could feel his heartbeat slowing as mine ratcheted up.

After what must have been a full minute, the man detached himself from me and latched onto Jake's lips. I watched as my husband's tension over the man's odd behavior eased away, too.

When the guy broke off after another long moment and took a step back, we all stood in the middle of the bar appraising one another. The stranger had a lump below his belt buckle, prominent even in the dim light. Yep, I realized, we were going to do this. Even if he became a problem, it would be two against one. For better or worse, this guy was leaving with us.

"You have an Orca card?" I asked.

The man frowned, reached into his pocket to be sure his wallet was still there, and nodded slowly.

"Are you up for two hours of sex and then cuddling through the night?" Jake asked.

The man closed his eyes and took a deep breath.

"Your name?" I prodded.

"Andy."

"Let's go make out on light rail, Andy, to stay in the mood until we get home." Jake pointed to the door, and our new acquaintance, after a brief hesitation, started off, glancing nervously over his shoulder. Our own nerves were tingling again, and we returned his unsettling glance.

Did I mention that there were *three* of us who experienced a psychotic break at the same time that night? It happened not long after we helped Andy into our sling.

Chapter Two: Jake

This next part is tricky. I'm helping Santino compile our account and am not quite sure I want researchers knowing the ins and outs (literally) of our sex lives. People either get disgusted for absolutely no reason or instead become unnecessarily titillated by the details, and those details are not really the point. Frankly, no matter how good the sex is, if you're not the one engaging in it, the specifics can get a bit tedious.

That said, it'll be hard to avoid all discussion of sex, given how the psychotic break developed.

"Condom?" Santino asked after rimming Andy in the sling for several minutes.

While reading about others having sex may not be fun, watching it take place in front of you most definitely is.

"Um..." Andy wriggled in the sling. His furry asshole reminded me of a FB meme showing a dog's ass that looked like an image of Jesus on toast.

"You on PrEP?" Santino clarified.

"I'm...uh...positive," Andy managed.

Santino and I were both negative, having successfully navigated quite the minefield in our early days. Some of our friends were still terrified of HIV but we'd learned long ago that with a few precautions, there was no need to consider poz men off limits. We'd both started PrEP six years earlier, after much discussion of side effects, and of course continued to use condoms when appropriate. After all, there were still plenty of other bugs we were happy to avoid. We were at the front of the line for the monkeypox vaccine.

But it was hard to suspect the world might be coming to an end—or at least our lives—and not want to live a little. Climate researchers had just revealed that every single day last year, the ocean set temperature records. There were nuclear threats from North Korea, Iran, and Russia. The upcoming Election Day renamed Christian Visibility Day. Santino and I took more risks than we should to enjoy the kind of sex we wanted. Not something we'd necessarily encourage others to do, but it was the decision we made for ourselves.

As gay men, as a non-monogamous couple, we were comfortable with being judged.

"We like fucking without condoms when we can," I jumped in, "but we're fine with putting one on if you'd rather." We tried *not* to judge others' boundaries. There were way too many to synchronize.

In college, for example, I'd written an essay on the "6 Best Uses for Cock." My professor had demanded I see him after class to discuss the inappropriateness of the topic. We discussed it several times during office hours and once at his home. At the end of the semester, he offered to give me an A, but I knew I'd only earned a B and insisted he assign me that instead.

Andy's brows furrowed at our simple question, and I exchanged a glance with Santino. We'd already whispered a few concerns regarding the guy's mental stability. He seemed unnaturally on edge. At least with him in the sling and his feet in stirrups, he'd be easier to control if he started behaving irrationally. We had padded handcuffs in a nearby drawer if necessary.

Hard to keep a hard on under these stressful conditions, but the dick pills helped. So did Andy's hairy butt.

Who didn't like seeing Jesus on toast?

"I want to feel you inside me," Andy finally said. "Not just latex. Human skin."

"We have lambskin, too," Santino offered.

Andy shook his head. "I want to feel *you*."

Santino applied some lube and slowly inserted a finger. After a few moments, I inserted a finger alongside his to help open Andy up.

There's nothing like sharing the rectum of a stranger to bring a couple closer.

Santino pounded him first and I followed right after. Those who have participated in multiple partner sex will understand when I say one of the best parts of being second (or third or fourth) when fucking a guy is not knowing how much of that slick feeling on your dick is the lube or another man's cum from a previous load.

TMI?

Okay. Back to the psychotic break.

Despite my earlier announcement that I longed for a two-hour session, Santino and I were both finished within twenty-five minutes. We managed to draw out Andy's orgasm another twenty, taking turns sucking his slightly curved cock. When the man finally came in my mouth, Santino and I stood on opposite sides of the sling, leaning over Andy to kiss, exchanging his cum and letting a little drip out of our mouths onto his chest.

Dang. Sorry. Can't help myself.

When Santino and I finally pulled apart, I leaned down to kiss Andy with the last bit of cum on my tongue but stopped when I realized he was crying.

"Oh my god," I said. "You okay?"

He shook his head, and I couldn't help noticing his ears. Lickable. Though we may have missed our chance if he was starting to freak out.

"What's wrong?" Santino looked at me nervously. Everyone knew that some closet case fundamentalists felt enormous guilt immediately after cumming.

"I'm dead." Andy began bawling outright, no longer sobbing quietly.

"Um…"

Perhaps this was his way of announcing clinical depression, I thought. Or a break up. Maybe he'd been fired from his job. Maybe the man had cancer or some other terminal disease.

Maybe he was upset over Lizzo announcing her retirement.

"I was afraid I'd never feel another man again," he choked out. "Never talk to another man. Never...never talk to *anyone* again."

The man wasn't putting us on. Something was up. He looked healthy enough physically, but evidently some neurons were misfiring. Santino and I had let our hormones take over, and we'd brought a problem home tonight. It was always a risk, of course. There'd been the guy who pissed all over our bed. The guy who sneaked off with a pewter gargoyle ring. And the guy who'd left a DVD of Jennifer Lopez's *Gigli*.

"Is there someone we can call?" I asked. His case worker? His psychiatrist?

He raised his arms in a gesture indicating he wanted help climbing out of the sling. After exchanging another nervous glance, Santino and I pulled him to his feet. Andy hugged me tightly for a moment and then Santino. He kissed us both and then hugged us again. He put his ear against my chest and listened to my heartbeat.

He sighed as if experiencing a second orgasm.

Santino and I stood motionless, unsure what to do. Andy moved to the chair where we'd placed his clothes and began rummaging. He was one of those guys whose dick was just as long flaccid as hard. Pulling out his phone, he scrolled through some text messages and held his phone out toward us.

"Andy, where are you?" read one.

"You're late! Call me!"

"You OK?"

"If you don't check in, I'm writing you up."

"Where the fuck are you?"

"You OK?"

Half a dozen similar texts followed. This guy had gone AWOL without telling his friends and supervisor at work. Mentally stable people didn't do things like that. I placed a hand on Santino's arm and carefully pulled him away.

I wanted to go home.

Oh, wait.

Andy made several more taps on his phone and then held it out for us again. Gently pushing Santino behind me, I approached to take a peek, seeing a news article about a man being found dead in an alley downtown.

It included a photo of a smiling Andy.

I'd watched reruns of *Candid Camera* as a kid, but prank shows these days came up with scenarios that weren't at all funny. Still, this set up seemed too bizarre even for that. What show was going to feature three naked men covered in the aftermath of sex when one of them suddenly shouts, "April Fool!"

"Watch," Andy said. He pulled up a text, clicked the Call icon next to it, and called the person who'd texted him. He held the phone out so we could hear it ring. And ring and ring.

"No voice mail," Andy pointed out. "No one ever answers and I can't leave a message. I can text back, but I can't tell if they receive it. No one ever responds."

"Um…"

"I've still got my house keys." Andy reached into his black jeans lying on the chair and pulled out a ring with a handful of keys. "I've been back. I can still log onto my computer. I can read emails, but when I respond, no one seems to receive them. I can look up news articles. I can watch YouTube videos." He closed his eyes and took a deep breath. "But I'm not really there."

"Andy," Santino began but then stopped. What was there to say? We couldn't really call the police for help. There was a reason community leaders wanted funds for mental health crisis first responders.

I nodded for my husband to start getting dressed. We might need to run out of our house in the middle of the night if the guy pulled a knife on us. Some of our neighbors were churchgoers, and streaking had gone out of fashion in the 1970s.

Of course, I knew that most mentally ill people were as harmless as anyone else.

Like folks who believed in Jewish space lasers. Or that alien lizard people ruled the country. Or that you could fund a functioning infrastructure without making the wealthy pay their fair share in taxes.

In other words, who really knew how dangerous this guy was?

"It's been *four* days," Andy continued. "You're the only people who can see me." He shook his head with a soft laugh. "I've been yelling in grocery stores and on buses and in hospitals and even at the police station. You don't know…" He caught himself choking and patted his chest. "You don't know what it's like to…to not matter." He turned away, and I could see his shoulders shake ever so slightly.

He wasn't laughing. This was a mentally disturbed man we needed to help. It wasn't the first time. You couldn't ride public transit regularly and not have to talk someone down once in a while. I moved over and put a hand on his trembling shoulder. "Is there someone we can call?" I asked again, so softly I could barely hear myself.

He shrugged, still turned away. "What could you say? 'Andy's ghost told me to tell you…'"

What in the world was happening? I thought about those shows like *Touched by an Angel*, where the angel had to convince someone they were real, and the non-angels always thought the angel was crazy or lying to them. Until a heavenly light appeared.

No light appeared.

"Do you…do you know who killed you?" Santino joined us and put a hand on Andy's other shoulder. I had no idea if he was humoring the guy or believed him. Santino read books about near-death experiences. He insisted we watch shows like *The Ghost Whisperer* and *Spirited*. He believed in an afterlife. I didn't.

Andy turned to face us. "The last thing I remember was having dinner with coworkers at a restaurant on Second Avenue. Then…nothing."

I remembered now hearing a snippet on the news about a man who'd been stabbed to death not far from the courthouse. The article Andy had showed us clicked into place. I'd assumed the man killed had been homeless. So many unhoused folks downtown these days. But maybe a homeless man had been the murderer, not the victim.

I wasn't sure which of my biases was more biased.

"Were you robbed?" I asked. I obviously didn't *believe* the guy. I was humoring him, too. Obviously.

"I still have my wallet and cards but the money's gone."

"A polite murderer?" Santino asked. "Wanted you to still have your ID when you were found?"

Andy shrugged again. "Just telling you what I know." He pointed to his clothes. "This isn't what I was wearing that night," he said. "I changed when I got home. But I still had my wallet on me after I woke up."

"And did you wake up in the alley?" Santino asked.

Andy shook his head. "I was sitting on a bench in Pioneer Square the next morning." He looked at us, his eyes pleading. "I know it doesn't make any sense." He absentmindedly began humming a tune I recognized as "If They Could See Me Now."

Jesus H. Christ. I'd read articles about mass hysteria. Discussing whether mental illness was contagious. What the hell were we going to do? "Listen, Andy," I began, rubbing the back of my head.

"Could you tell if anyone else at the bar saw me?" he interrupted. "Anyone?" When we didn't answer, he answered his own question. "Nope."

"Well, we weren't really paying attention," Santino pointed out. "We were looking at the cute guy standing on the table."

"With one button of his fly undone," I added, "right at eye level."

For the first time since we'd finished up at the sling, Andy smiled. But his smile only lasted an instant. "I hope you *keep* seeing me," he whispered. "I don't want to disappear again."

Whenever pundits discussed the possibility of UFOs and claimed that the government was hiding the truth because people couldn't handle learning something so unsettling, I often yelled at the television. "People will get over it in two days! We adapt quickly! Tell us if there's something out there!"

And after only a few minutes, Andy's claims seemed almost possible, even without the heavenly glow.

Santino put his arms around the man and hugged him tightly. "If there's a reason we can see you when no one else can," he said, "we'll make sure that reason only gets stronger."

There was sure a reason I loved Santino.

"Do you think ghosts can cum twice?" Andy asked shyly.

I looked at Santino and shrugged before turning back to our murdered friend. "I suppose there's only one way to find out."

Santino was half dressed but began removing his clothes again. This time, I climbed into the sling, offering up my ass to a dead man and putting his slightly overgrown beard to good use.

I sent up a silent thanks to Sue Ann Nivens for giving us the idea to put a mirror on the ceiling of our playroom.

Now the psychotic break was final. All three of us believed the same, ridiculous delusion.

The problem was, of course, that once you genuinely believe a delusion, it no longer feels ridiculous. You simply start living your life as if it's all true.

But doing so, as you can imagine, can still create a host of unexpected, unmitigated disasters.

Chapter Three: Andy

These two gullible dweebs, I realized, were absolutely bonkers. What kind of freaks would believe a story like the one I'd just told?

Sexy freaks, for sure, but then, I'd had more than my share of freaky sex over the years. Good sex, even assuming I was up to snuff that evening, wouldn't account for how quickly they'd accepted my story. Perhaps they were on drugs, I thought. Maybe someone had slipped something into their drinks before they spotted me in the bar.

Perhaps they were dead, too.

Santino and Jake have convinced me they couldn't write this account without my input, and I suppose I see their point, so I'm doing what I can. Of course, one of them needs to read what I've written on my laptop and then retype it into their own document, since nothing I write seems visible to anyone besides them.

They're editing as they go, completely erasing my voice. It's a bit patronizing, but whatever. It's not as if word choice and cadence are the point of the project. And we seem to think an awful lot alike in any event.

Is that why they can see me?

There were no researchers to ask. What terms could you put in the Search bar? Watching reruns of Hope Lange in *The*

Ghost and Mrs. Muir didn't help. Which Jake and Santino have insisted on regardless.

Though it was fun to watch an apparently out actor in the series. In 1968, for God's sake. Before Stonewall.

Could you really be invisible if you avoided saying the wrong word?

When Santino and Jake proposed the project, I insisted they not actually send it to anyone when we finished. They'd end up institutionalized for sure, and even though I could probably tag along, it was hardly where any of us would find happiness. At the very least, they'd be put on meds that might negate any possibility of a sex life. They could even be separated, and I'd need to go back and forth between rooms or even buildings. Since I couldn't walk through walls, *any* kind of imprisonment would be problematic.

"What if someone finds this?" I asked. The police, a family member, a friend.

"We'll pretend it's a novel," Santino assured me.

"Shouldn't we use fake names?"

So Jake, Santino, and Andy aren't our real names. We'll pretend we're "basing" the story on the news report of the murder near Pioneer Square and then simply made up all the rest.

Still, I'm worried. My life—or existence—has been compromised enormously. I don't want anything terrible to happen to Jake and Santino as well. If fascists do take over in November, even a novel about gay threesomes, with or without sex scenes, will probably get them incarcerated. Just the other day, some right-wing nutjob in Oklahoma proposed a bill that would label sexting and sexual selfies as porn, then label sending those pics or sexual messages as "distribution of pornography." Anyone not the recipient of such messages but who was aware of them could then sue the sender for $10,000. And these crimes would be punishable by twenty years in prison.

This was the world we might be living in even if fascists *didn't* take over in November.

One didn't need to die to go to hell.

And it seemed we were all in limbo right now.

In any event, I agreed to take part in the writing.

After that second round of sex, we headed to Jake and Santino's bedroom and climbed into bed, with me in the middle, all spooning. To be honest, I was afraid to close my eyes, worried I'd never wake up, cease existing altogether. But their warm bodies felt too comforting. I'd been under such stress the previous few days and couldn't keep myself from dozing off.

When I awakened later, it took a moment to remember where I was. Then I felt so happy I almost squealed in joy. Almost all of us take waking up for granted. We take being with people we love or at least like for granted. Even for couples who remain madly in love, there will come a day when only one of them wakes up in the morning.

This wasn't that day, and it was *fabulous*.

Then a new problem arose. I had to pee. Clearly, bodily functions still functioned, or I'd never have been able to cum the night before. I tried to extricate myself from Jake's arms.

"Mmmm," he moaned pleasantly. "Good morning."

"Hey there."

"You still dead?"

"Afraid so."

Jake pulled my head toward him and gave me a peck. "Sorry for the morning breath," he said.

"You'll be a lot sorrier if I don't get to the bathroom," I replied. "My bladder is about to burst."

"Huh?" Santino mumbled into his pillow. "What was that?" He turned around and faced me, growing fully alert within seconds. "Bathroom's that way." He pointed.

I hadn't finished when the two of them joined me beside the bowl, all of us pissing at the same time. I felt like one of Macbeth's witches.

[I should note that I did not write that last sentence. Jake and Santino are using a heavy hand editing this draft. I find it a bit insulting, but what am I gonna do? Take 'em to court? I'll probably just fuck them with a little less sphincter prep tonight.]

[I expect my critique will be edited out of the next draft. Santino said he's trying to confuse any computer analysis done on our report by blending our voices, though I'm not sure that'll be possible. AI is pretty good these days.]

[Oh my goodness! Am I a computer simulation? Or am I real and everyone *else* a simulation?]

I never pissed alongside any of my previous partners. Our rare ventures into watersports took place in the shower. Once in a family member's swimming pool. But don't tell Kathy.

Kathy's brother, Roland, was my latest ex, the only partner I was ever legally married to, and he couldn't see me anymore. I'd checked. He'd been a jealous mutherfucker and smothered our love with his suspicions and accusations. I'd never once cheated on him, but he'd given me the cold shoulder if I was even fifteen minutes late from work.

"They're called quickies for a reason," he'd say every time and then not speak to me for the rest of the evening. Sometimes, when I was in the mood for some alone time, I'd deliberately come home late. But the misery was never worth it.

We'd broken up a month ago. The divorce wasn't final, but really, who cared at this point? He could have whatever he wanted from the house. I'd already sneaked out a few ghost copies of my favorite books. To everyone else's eyes, they'd still be sitting about my former home, but I couldn't access them unless I felt them in my hands. Perhaps now that I had a couple of allies, I should move some tangible things over here.

"It's Saturday," Santino said, shaking the last drop from his dick. "Should we make plans for the day?" He frowned. "I'm not really sure how to handle…" He motioned to the air all around us.

"I want to find out who killed me," I said. "I mean, I enjoyed last night, but what if I fade away tomorrow? Or today? I have no idea why I'm even still here at all, so I could evaporate at any minute."

I wanted to say more, but in the daylight, every word sounded preposterous. If I'd still been alive, maybe I'd have run into Santino and Jake at the bar anyway now that I was single. We might still have ended up together. Friends? Sex buddies? A permanent threesome? But it could never last under the current circumstances. We'd never be able to go to a restaurant together without them looking insane. We could never hang out with friends. At best, I'd be a kept boy, hidden in a closet when guests came over.

At worst, Jake and Santino would come to their senses, kick me out, and I'd become a homeless ghost.

"Have you read the police report?" Jake asked. "You said you've been to the police station."

I nodded before we headed back to the bedroom and began dressing. "Takes some patience, since I can't turn the pages or scroll on my own or ask questions. Nada."

Yeah, I know. I can touch and move things here, so why not there? Why could I climb onto a table in the bar but not be able to use a mouse at the police station?

Reruns of *My Mother, the Car* didn't help explain much, either.

[I didn't write that, but I'll take credit for it because they seem to know their trivia.]

[Sheesh, and now they've edited my commentary.]

"What do the police know so far?" Santino put his hand on my arm, probably assuring himself he wasn't seeing things, but also probably deciding I was just some jerk pulling his leg, after all.

"I'd gone to dinner with my boss and a few coworkers. We did it once a month. It was supposedly voluntary, but you could tell my manager wouldn't look kindly on absences."

"Union job?" Jake asked.

I shook my head. "Mortgage department. My manager Bouchra was there, my coworkers Marilyn, Wickens, and Brett. A new part-timer, too."

"Nothing unusual?" Jake motioned for us to follow him to the kitchen, where he put on a pot of coffee as we continued chatting. He made some toast using keto bread and what looked like butter made from cashews.

"No arguing, if that's what you mean. I don't like my boss and she doesn't like me. Wickens is a born again Christian, so I keep my distance, but he's never said anything mean to me. Given me the stink eye a few times, but in a work setting, who hasn't?"

"Wickens?" Santino asked.

"We're not really on a first-name basis."

"Any anti-gay stuff at work?"

I shrugged. "Not specifically. Marilyn's passive aggressive, but I don't know her politics."

"And Brett?" Santino asked.

I felt my face flush. "Brett propositioned me a few times. Wasn't happy when I told him I was monogamous. Wasn't happy after my breakup with Roland when I said I needed some down time."

"And Roland?" Jake pressed.

I caught them up to speed on that situation. We sat at the kitchen table, munching in silence. Santino poured us each a second cup of coffee while Jake handed out one strawberry for each of us.

"You guys eat pretty light," I noted.

Jake patted his stomach. "You'd never know."

"Maybe you'd be thirty pounds heavier if you didn't."

"Don't depress me."

"You're asking a dead guy?"

After we finished the last of our breakfast, I picked up the cups to wash in the sink. I noticed an ant on the windowsill and instinctively moved to squash it but then stopped myself.

No squashing today.

"Does the same group meet every month?" Santino asked. "Anyone there who didn't usually participate? Anyone missing this time?"

I considered a moment as I set the cups in the drainboard. "Petar's a part-timer. He's new."

"Did you deny any loans recently?" asked Santino. "Foreclose on anyone?"

"I'm not a loan officer," I said. "Not even a processor."

"What do you do?"

"I maintain the files."

"What the hell does that mean?" Jake demanded.

"It means if I hadn't been murdered, I'd probably have ended up killing myself from sheer boredom."

There was silence in the kitchen for a long moment.

"You know," I picked up the conversation after the tension grew too thick, "if my murder was random, you guys are probably safe because there's no way you'll find him." I paused. "But if I was targeted and you try to find the killer, he might come after you, too." Hardly the best way to defuse the tension, I realized a moment later.

I could see in their eyes they understood the additional ramifications. Not everyone might come back as ghosts, and even if they did, all ghosts might not end up in the same place. Whether or not they'd miss being with me after such a brief time was one thing, but they might not be with each other, either.

Chapter Four: Santino

"So," I said, "it's Saturday. We have the weekend off. Is there anything we can do today to help?"

Andy scrunched his nose in thought. "Roland's moved out of the house into an apartment. But we both own the place. If he hasn't moved back in yet, he will soon."

"Nice of him to move out rather than demand you move," I said.

"He said he didn't want to go to jail and didn't think he could keep from hitting me if he stayed one minute longer."

"We should question him," Jake decided.

Andy nodded slowly. "He can be a real jerk," he admitted, "but he wasn't all bad. I wouldn't have been with him if he was a jerk every second of the day. Everyone's a mixed bag."

I shrugged. "Some mixed bags have a smaller variety of nuts than others." I paused. "And some nuts are rotten."

"I suppose anything's possible. Spouses and exes are prime suspects in most murders, aren't they?"

"You think he'll attack us when we ask him awkward questions?" Jake rubbed the back of his head.

"He'll yell for sure. He's good at that. But I do want you to pick up a few more of my things. He hates my dragon chess pieces. He'll start throwing stuff out soon."

I raised my eyebrows. "Mourning period of five days?"

"He was angry. And if he didn't take his anger out on my body, he'll take it out on my favorite belongings."

"Mixed bag, huh?"

Jake clapped once, loudly, startling both of us. "No time like the present," he said. "Where do you live?"

"West Seattle. My car got towed but Roland drove it back to the house. Do you guys want to start driving it?"

How could we possibly explain taking Andy's car to Roland, I wondered, or to the police or anyone else? Besides, neither Jake nor I had driven in many years, both to save money and to advocate for public transit. Neither of us would feel comfortable behind the wheel. We passed on the offer.

"You want to call a rideshare?" Andy asked.

"We'd better go by bus," Jake said.

"You guys are into S&M?"

"We're saving the planet." Jake motioned toward the window with a practiced Vanna White move.

"Can you postpone carbon dioxide anxiety for a few days?"

"Well, we don't want a record of being driven to your house, do we?"

"Ugh." I groaned. "West Seattle. That's what? Three? Four buses? Can we at least catch a rideshare back?"

"Is my being butchered in the prime of my life inconveniencing you?"

"A little."

"Ah, you guys are killing me."

"Too late."

Ten minutes later, we stood at the bus stop on Renton Avenue, waiting for the 106. A series of twenty or more earthen mounds protruded out of the parking strip a couple of feet apart, crossing under the sidewalk and heading diagonally across someone's yard, a dotted line that had gone off course.

Moles.

Last week in Kubota Garden, we'd watched a bald eagle swoop down and grab an orange and black koi out of the pond. Just the other day, Jake and I had watched two raccoons fighting in our front yard, in broad daylight.

It was difficult not to be impressed with these up close and personal sightings, no matter how problematic they might be. The Pacific Northwest was a lovely place.

I hoped if we were put into concentration camps next year, they'd be somewhere around here. Most of the Japanese Americans from Seattle, including the Kubotas, had ended up in the desert near Minidoka, Idaho. Others from the area had been taken to internment camps in the California desert.

The air was cool and crisp today, clear enough we could just make out Mount Baker in the distance. Time to focus.

"What'll we say if Roland's at your place?" I asked.

Andy shrugged. "That you're coworkers?" he suggested. "Cousins? Detectives?" He grunted. "We'll think of something. If he's home, we'll question him. If he's not, we'll grab my things."

The bus pulled up a moment later and we climbed aboard, choosing two empty seats just ahead of the rear exit because they offered the most leg room, and we felt it best if Andy sat on my lap. Too unnerving to have him sit in a separate seat and then watch someone sit on top of him.

Would their images blend together? Could he possess someone?

Perhaps he'd be like a fly on the wall, observing but not able to interact with whoever he was inside. Or would the combination of two souls cause some kind of short circuit and fry the living person's brain?

What if Andy got trapped inside someone and couldn't ever get back out? Like being awake during surgery but unable to move or to scream that you could still feel the scalpel?

A homeless man lay across three seats in the Disability section of the bus. He was a white guy, maybe in his mid-thirties, wearing stained clothes, hugging a dirty blanket. He coughed, sat up, and blew his nose into his hands. Then he used the mucus like gel as he ran his fingers through his sandy blond hair.

I thought about Cameron Diaz.

Jake and I still wore our N94s on transit.

The man continued coughing for the next twenty minutes, kept blowing his nose into his hands and using his mucus as gel. When he finally got up to leave, we could see the back of his pants were soaked across his ass and halfway down his legs.

Andy shifted on my lap, turning to address Jake and me. "I don't know where I'll go next," he said, his voice shaking slightly, "but I doubt I'll have it as bad as that guy does right now."

An hour and a half after we left our house, we stepped off the bus in West Seattle. As we followed Andy, he pointed in disgust at what first appeared to be an award-winning mid-century property.

His?

The bright green yard was immaculate, every bush trimmed to perfection, bordered by a line of black mondo grass. The cream paint on the home's siding was pristine, the windows glistening and clean. A dead crow hung upside down by a metal wire from the upper branches of a carefully manicured Japanese pine.

A warning to other crows. A home of practiced, cultivated cruelty. Was this Roland's doing?

"Hatred for survivors of the dinosaur apocalypse," Andy muttered. "I realize most people complain about the folks who don't keep up their property. But sometimes, it's the folks that do who are the bigger problem."

So *not* Roland's work. "You argue with the owner?"

Andy shrugged. "After I asked him to take down the first dead bird he hung up there, I found it on our front steps the next morning."

"Charming."

"We mostly ignore him now," he continued. "Except for Christmas when he hangs several of those things from the damn tree."

"No special Christmas desserts?" Jake asked. "Four and twenty blackbirds baked in a pie?"

Andy stopped in his tracks and turned toward us. "He did bring us some homemade burritos once," he said. "I wouldn't eat them but Roland had one." His eyes narrowed as he remembered. "Got food poisoning, now that I think of it."

"You didn't notice your neighbor in the restaurant that night, did you?" I asked. "Run into him by chance on the street?"

Andy frowned, thinking hard, but eventually shook his head. "I honestly can't remember. Maybe I'm blocking terrible memories."

"Sounds like you remember some pretty bad ones," Jake noted.

We continued walking, and soon Andy motioned to an older home. "My car's here." He pointed. "But Roland's isn't." They owned a Craftsman, too, but not like ours, theirs an impressive two-story structure in fine condition. Andy's home featured a porch with tapered columns while ours had the more pedestrian, straight ones. His also had a prominent, tapered chimney, distinct to the period. We'd lost part of ours in the 2001 earthquake and removed the rest since we weren't using it, anyway. Over twenty years and we still hadn't finished the necessary home improvements.

A tear down when we bought it, we'd slowly put in energy efficient windows. And insulation. The house had none in either the ceiling or the walls when we bought it. But the place was far from finished. Moss on the roof, peeling paint on the siding. It wasn't that we didn't have savings, but as retirement age approached, we were all too aware they wouldn't last long.

Jake and I were running out of time to make any more repairs. Our bodies wouldn't hold out forever, whether or not our money or freedoms did.

I'd seen a video the other day of a prominent right-wing conservative bragging about how he gave fake money to homeless people, hoping they'd get caught by the police. Jake and I had far more than the basics and nothing to complain about, with or without a perfect house.

Andy pulled out his key, opened the door, and punched in the alarm code.

We should probably get a security system one of these days, too.

A GOP senate candidate in Arizona had recently encouraged all MAGA supporters to start packing a Glock as the election season ramped up. At a rally a few days ago, Trump predicted a "bloodbath" if he didn't win. A national security official explained to a journalist that it wasn't a matter of "if" there'd be violence after the election in November. It was inevitable, no matter who won. What we needed to do was be prepared to mitigate it.

An alarm code might not be the protection it used to be.

I hugged Andy, then Jake, and we started moving slowly about the house.

"What do you want to us to pack first?" Jake asked. We'd brought two cloth bags each, large enough to hold several changes of clothes. We'd have to walk a few blocks from the house before calling a rideshare service so our location would be less trackable. If we took only a few bags worth of items, Roland might not even notice someone had been here.

We could come back another time to question him.

"I suppose there's no point taking things we can replace," Andy mused. "But I want a couple of photo albums, the DVD I made of me having sex with my first partner, an original painting of two cowboys by a gay artist I met once in New Mexico, and a patchwork quilt I made of three men sucking each other at the same time."

"Prescient."

"I think the word is 'prurient.'"

"We'll grab the hard copy of my address book so you guys can contact people for me."

"You've really thought about this."

"Have a lot of free time now that I'm out of work."

I was beginning to feel the effects of my enlarged prostate and headed to the bathroom for a quick break. These guys sure kept their place cleaner than Jake and I did. I made sure to wipe up any stray drops. The older I got, the more my stream seemed to diverge into multiple streams. There were exceptionally few situations where wide-spraying urine was a plus. I flushed and then went to the sink to wash my hands.

"Shit!" I knocked the soap dispenser into the sink.

"You okay?" Jake called out from the bedroom.

"Yep. All good." I turned and looked behind me. No one there. But I could have sworn I'd seen a bear of a man. Tall, unrealistically muscular, with a beard any of the three of us would die for.

Hmm. I looked up into the corners of the room. Maybe…

"Is someone there?" I whispered. "I can't see you anymore. Can you hear me?" What did one say to…no one? "Can you move something?"

Apparently not.

"We, uh, have no problem with ghosts," I said. "As long as you're a good ghost."

Was this someone else Roland had murdered? Did this mean he really was Andy's killer? I felt dizzy and braced myself against the counter.

I felt like an idiot. I still wasn't sure, after all, that Jake and I weren't experiencing a psychotic break. But whatever I'd seen, real or imagined, didn't return, so I dried my hands and joined the others.

We spent the next twenty minutes packing quickly but carefully, finding we had room to throw in Andy's chaps, a leather wrist band, and a handful of sex toys. We really were a good bit alike. Just as we were heading for the exit, we heard a key rattle in the front door.

"Uh oh."

It was Saturday, after all. Probably not the best day to have chosen if we wanted to go undetected.

A moment later, we were face to face with Roland Kronenberg. Almost six feet tall, he wore running shorts that revealed perfectly proportioned legs. His T-shirt read, "Takes One to Know One." I supposed that applied to pretty much any taunt.

"Who the fuck are you?" he demanded. We were clearly holding stolen items after breaking into his home and he didn't even feel threatened. Rather insulting.

"We're friends of Andy's," I managed. "He…uh…left us a list of items he wanted to donate to an LGBTQ archive."

Roland's eyes narrowed. "Are you taking *my* things?" He glared at our bags as if they might wilt under his gaze and confess.

"Andy's happy for you to have the house and everything else in it," Jake said, "but he wants us to donate these specific items."

I raised one of the bags.

"Like hell."

"I'm afraid these were Andy's wishes," I repeated.

"You have that in writing?" Roland demanded. "*I* have his will. And—hey! Were you guys *fucking* my husband!? How come I don't know you? Did he give you our key? Have you been fucking in *our* bed!?"

"You'd better call 9-1-1," Andy muttered. "He's about to start throwing things."

If we called the police, we'd never get away with Andy's prized possessions. Perhaps we could pay his ex for them.

So much for saving money by taking the bus here.

But when I saw Roland pick up a ceramic vase, I pulled out my phone. "9-1-1," a calm female voice said a moment later. "What is your emergency?"

"I'm at the home of Andrew Frey. He was murdered last week. His ex, Roland Kronenberg, is threatening me and may have killed Andy in a jealous rage. Please send someone."

Andy waved the vase like a lasso he was about to let loose. I held one arm up as a shield just in case.

It was impossible not to have watched the news over the past few years and not be painfully aware that calling the police could lead to premature death for innocent people. Or even for guilty people who still didn't deserve the death penalty. Every few weeks, some online publication posted another article on "7 Things to Stay Safe When You're Stopped by the Police." Jake and I were the intruders here, after all, yet we didn't want Roland to be hurt, either.

"I didn't kill Andy!" Roland hissed. "He lied about being married, didn't he? You were pissed when you found out. *You* killed him!"

The vase just missed me, hitting Andy on the shoulder, bouncing off and striking a lamp beside him. Roland blinked.

I had no idea which metaphysical rules were at play.

When the police arrived, we all raised our hands until the officers felt comfortable there was no real danger. Having seen way too many bodycam videos showing officers shooting unarmed people posing no possible threat whatsoever, my heart was still beating furiously even after they put their weapons away.

"So Roland *can* control his temper when he wants to," Andy noted.

"Shh!" I hissed.

"Excuse me?" One of the officers cast a surly look in my direction.

"I sneezed."

Jake rubbed the back of his head.

Apparently, because of my accusations during the 9-1-1 call, the officers were told to keep us under control until the detectives assigned to investigate Andy's murder arrived. At least that meant the department was still investigating. Resources were limited, after all, and gay men couldn't be that high on their priority list. Just last year, after a police officer struck and killed a young Indian woman in a crosswalk, a leader in the police union was caught on audio saying the woman's life was of "limited value."

"I'm sorry I got you guys into this mess," Andy whispered. "None of my stuff is important enough to put up with Roland."

Jake and I obviously couldn't respond.

"He was like this even with me," Andy went on. He shook his head and gave a disgusted snort. "More and more lately. I already donated my expensive breakables to friends and family and even a couple of organizations. It's painful to watch a Val St. Lambert vase explode into a hundred pieces."

I'd have to take his word on that.

Maybe if we weren't arrested, and we were all still together at Christmas—and hadn't been murdered by Christian nationalists—Jake and I could save up and buy something nice for Andy.

"I wasted so much of my life with this guy." He closed his eyes, his voice catching. "It wasn't all bad, like I said, and I'm glad I finally left, but I sure wish I'd done it sooner."

"We love you, Andy," I said softly. "Everything's going to be okay."

Everyone turned to stare, but fortunately, right at that moment, the detectives arrived.

Chapter Five: Jake

Detective Gamroth, a strawberry blonde in her late thirties, seemed to be the senior, Detective Degroen, a stout, clean-shaven man in his mid-forties her junior.

Stout was easier to pull off when accompanied by a beard.

Of course, with microplastics in our food supply killing off yet more of the good bacteria in our guts, we'd all probably need to reset to Rubenesque beauty standards sooner rather than later.

I barely registered the woman's physical girth. It simply didn't matter to me. But I pretty much evaluated every man on a variety of scales—facial attractiveness, facial hair, hair color, body type, weight, and how well they wore their clothing. The style of clothing mattered less.

With so many parameters, you'd think it inevitable a guy would score low in one category or another. But my scale wasn't exclusionary. No matter how many low scores a man might register, it was almost certain he'd score well at least once.

And that was all it took to find him attractive.

Degroen had nice ears. Okay, that was a bit of a stretch. But ears were as distinct as fingerprints, even without jewelry or gauging. Degroen's had lobes the right size for nibbling, an entrance to the ear canal just right for sticking my tongue into. I could imagine looking at his ears from behind as I—

"Mr. Maddox?" a voice interrupted me. "Mr. Maddox?"

It was Detective Gamroth. "Excuse me," I said sheepishly. She was lightly freckled and made no attempt to hide it with makeup. Good for you, I thought.

As if my opinion on someone else's appearance mattered. Ever. Much less at a time like this.

I rubbed the back of my head.

"Who are you and why are you here?" she asked. She moved about slowly, looking here and there, observing everything, but her attention never seemed divided. She was listening and observing us more than anything else.

I repeated the same story we'd told Roland. Detective Gamroth's face looked expressionless and skeptical at the same time. Degroen jotted down some notes. He seemed distracted by Gamroth's ass.

Or maybe she had something on the back of her uniform.

"Give her the alarm code," Andy whispered, though there was hardly any need. Everyone else seemed oblivious to his presence. Even Roland couldn't be faking not seeing him. "It'll show you knew me." He spouted off the number and I repeated it.

"Andy wanted us to get these few items," Santino said. "He loved Roland but couldn't bear to live with him anymore because of his temper. He was fine with Roland keeping most things, but he wanted *these items* to go to a gay archive." He motioned to the bags we'd set aside.

"Tell her I don't think Roland killed me."

"I said what I did in the 9-1-1 call just to make sure someone came out fast," I admitted. "Because Roland does have a temper. But we don't think he had anything to do with Andy's death."

Roland was still in the same room, on the other side, talking to the officers who'd arrived first, and glaring daggers in our direction. But those runner's legs. Damn.

Detective Gamroth turned to see what I was seeing and then turned back to me, the corners of her mouth quirked up ever so slightly.

I wasn't sure she'd be as amused if she realized the way her partner was looking at her backside. But then, they were both forcing me to recognize my own inappropriate behavior.

"How did you know Mr. Frey?" Detective Degroen asked. The lead detective didn't seem to mind him asking questions of his own. But why would she? Santino and I watched detective shows all the time, and suddenly I couldn't recall the dynamics of detective interaction from a single one of them.

Why was the back of my head so itchy? Did I have dandruff?

"People don't hand out their security code to just anyone," he pointed out.

"Um…" Santino mumbled.

"You're going to have to tell them we had sex," Andy whispered. "I hate to let Roland think I cheated on him. He'll never trust anyone again. But the detectives aren't going to believe anything else."

"Roland's never going to trust anyone, anyway," I said. The brows on both detectives' faces lifted in unison. "We met Andy in a bar," I went on. "Took him home with us."

Santino closed his eyes, shaking his head.

"Is that not accurate, Mr. Castellano?"

"Yeah, that's what happened."

"If it'll help speeds things up," I said, "you're welcome to search our house." I'd read several articles advising folks never to allow a search without a warrant, never even to talk to police if it could be avoided, and to have an attorney present for any questioning. All likely good advice, even for folks who were 100% innocent. But human nature being what it was—irrational—I felt our best chance was being cooperative. After all, we didn't have anything to hide.

Famous last words.

And, to paraphrase Bill Clinton, it depended on your definition of "anything."

"Can we open the bags and show you and Roland what we were going to take?" Santino asked.

Detective Gamroth motioned for Roland to approach, and we proceeded to do just that. I couldn't help but notice Degroen standing slightly back, ostensibly to take notes, but occasionally stealing another glance at Gamroth's ass.

Stakeouts must be excruciating for them both, I thought, for entirely different reasons.

"You're telling me a gay archive wants Andy's dragons?" He crossed his arms. "And his *used* double-ended dildo?" Roland's lip curled in disgust.

"Different archives want different things," was all I could manage. "And I don't think any of your DNA is still present."

Detective Gamroth's lips quirked upward again. Detective Degroen's did not.

"Researchers may want to study the wear pattern on his blow job knee pads."

Detective Gamroth coughed. Degroen jotted down a note. Forcefully.

We had a bit of difficulty justifying Andy's favorite shirts, saying instead he'd been wearing them the few times we met, and we wanted something to remember him by. At this, Roland threw up his hands. "Fine!" he spat. "Take it all. Just get out and never come back. I'm changing the alarm code as soon as you get the fuck out of here."

I looked to Detective Gamroth, who shrugged. Then I motioned to Santino, and we repacked as quickly as possible, lugging the four cloth bags out front and to the sidewalk. Detective Gamroth said she'd be in contact with us later.

"Can we call a rideshare *now*?" Santino asked.

You'd think we'd wait until we got home before discussing the situation openly. After all, the rideshare driver wasn't an inanimate object. He could hear and think and feel. He could worry about the crazy people in his personal vehicle.

But our lives were quickly becoming like those of the residents in a *Big Brother* episode. You could realize there were cameras everywhere filming every interaction, but after a while, you forgot and just lived your life regardless.

"That went about as well as could be expected," Andy said.

"Oh my god," Santino spluttered. "You were expecting something *worse*, and you still had us go over there?"

"No one's dead." He shrugged. "Well, no one *else*. We got my things, and I feel even more convinced Roland had nothing to do with my murder."

"Is narrowing down the suspects at the bank going to be this traumatic?" Santino demanded.

"Well, Wickens can drone on a bit. That's why I wear the leather wrist bands. Decreases the risk of suicide."

"Anything else we should know?"

"Brett will probably make a pass at you."

"You okay with watching?" Santino asked.

"The propositioning? Or the sex?"

"Do they make three-ended dildos?" I interrupted. "Because if we're going to remain a threesome…"

The driver looked into his rearview mirror, checking the traffic behind us.

"I think we're all getting a better sense of how short life is," Santino said, reaching over to grasp our hands. "Sometimes, I feel a hundred years old and other times I wonder how all that time escaped without me noticing."

"We're at that age where we could live in good health another twenty years," I said, "or get diagnosed with cancer next week."

"Or, God forbid, dementia."

The driver looked in his rearview mirror again. His ears weren't so bad, either.

Two days ago, it would've taken a miracle for me to hire a rideshare driver. Someone in the news was always saying, "Life turns on a dime," but until it happened, you expected to keep going on pretty much the same every day. Dimes were for other people, those people who were always saying they expected overnight changes to happen to someone else.

And compared to what others were facing right now…

"Before we met you," I said, "we were planning to go to the Gaza protest this weekend out by the Museum of History and Industry. We can still make the tail end of it."

"If we take another rideshare."

"I think Andy's right on that score."

Last weekend, protesters had blocked the Golden Gate Bridge, the road in front of SeaTac airport, a road in front of

Chicago's O'Hare, and several other roads and bridges across the country. A far-right senator from Arkansas encouraged people to "take matters into their own hands" and throw protesters off bridges. If their hands were glued to the road, they should rip their skin off to force protesters away.

Over two hundred aid workers and ninety-seven journalists had been killed in Gaza in the past seven months, more than in any war of the same magnitude and duration. Newspapers reported more than 33,000 Palestinians killed so far, but the number was probably closer to 60,000. It was just that so many doctors, nurses, and others who could offer an official tally had also been targeted, with too many bodies still under the rubble left uncounted.

While teachers, journalists, and others in the U.S. and Europe were being fired for using the word "genocide."

I imagined dead Palestinians trudging across the desert toward the Knesset. Wouldn't *that* make an interesting *Walking Dead* spin off? Or Native American ghosts making the trek back east along the Trail of Tears?

Kirsten Dunst was starring in a movie right now called *Civil War*, about the violence threatening to overtake the U.S. Would vigilantes be hunting down gays? Blacks? Latinos?

It couldn't *really* happen here, could it? I mean, not *again*.

But isn't that what they thought in Syria? In Lebanon?

"Do you guys protest every weekend?" Andy asked.

I shook my head. "I've been to maybe six protests so far."

"I've been to eight," Santino offered.

"It's petty to feel inconvenienced by 'losing' four hours of my weekend when it's such a privileged position to be in," I said. "But the truth is, I do feel inconvenienced, and I don't go to every protest." Not even most.

"I rallied at two Gaza protests," Andy said. "The one at the King Street train station and one at light rail in the U District."

"Dammit. We didn't go to either of those." I squeezed Andy's hand. "Would've been nice to find a picture online we were all in together."

"You up for this?" Santino asked. "It's not as if you don't have pressing concerns of your own."

He shrugged again. "I can safely say I have no worries about being arrested today."

I snorted and then pulled Andy over for a kiss. The car swerved slightly and I sat back. Our driver's hands gripped the steering wheel tightly.

We dropped the bags off at the house, called a new rideshare driver, and grabbed our signs. "Stop military aid to Israel" and "End apartheid," with similar sayings on the back. You couldn't really say everything necessary in six words or less.

Santino and I participated in climate protests, too, and protests for reproductive rights, in support of barista unions. There were too many battles these days. The far right were pros at wearing people down. I felt tired now just thinking about all the things I *wasn't* doing.

We passed a formerly empty lot filled now with tiny homes for the unhoused, freshly painted in cheerful blues, reds, and yellows. Then a row of dented campers and RVs destitute people called home.

In a grocery store parking lot sat a jumble of at least six mattresses piled on top of two stained sofas, an easy chair with a broken back, and a shredded cat tower. For some reason, a metal grate painted white, in what appeared to be perfect condition, had been set atop one of the sofas.

"Life sucks sometimes," Andy whispered, looking out the window. "No doubt about it. But I still wish…"

I thought about Israel's attack on Iranian military leaders at a consulate in Damascus, Iran's counterattack with drones, and Israel's vow to "retaliate."

I thought about the huge subset of Christians salivating at the prospect of Armageddon. It was almost as if they were worshipping Anubis or the Morrigan rather than the Prince of Peace. Apocalypse lust.

Apocalypse porn was not a turn-on for me.

If there was an afterlife, though, if perhaps Andy would find himself in heaven next week, was death really a "bad" thing?

Even apocalyptic Christians—and Jews and Muslims, for that matter—had been given the commandment not to kill.

Was I wrong to hope there was a hell? Maybe not one that lasted for eternity, perhaps instead something like forcing the cruel to watch *Two Broke Girls* on a loop until they understood how the suffering they'd inflicted on others had harmed them.

"Remember Mila?" I asked. A friend we used to play darts with ages ago who'd died of ovarian cancer.

"I'm thinking about lots of people we've lost over the years."

We *had* lived through the AIDS crisis, after all. And COVID.

"When I think ahead to this November, I feel I'm hearing a doctor tell me I've got six to eight months left." Both Andy and Santino turned toward me. Our new driver looked in her rearview mirror. "I mean, you never really know for sure, do you? We had another friend diagnosed with terminal cancer four years ago—"

"Craig."

"Who's still doing reasonably well. But..."

Andy took up the thread now. "But getting a heads up at least gives you a chance to use your remaining time wisely, doesn't it? To live whatever time you have left a bit more consciously."

"Because you might only have *three* months left," I continued, "and not even six." I took a long moment to look at Andy. In terms of "traditional beauty" he was probably a 7.5 or an 8. Only movie stars and models generally rated a 9 or a 10. So Andy was way above average, even with the paunch. But now that we knew him, he looked like an 11 to me.

And someone had murdered him.

Soldiers were killing civilians in Gaza. Police were imprisoning LGBTQ folks in Russia and Uganda and Nigeria and Saudi Arabia and elsewhere. Civil war was still raging in Sudan.

"There's such a thing as a self-fulfilling prophecy," Santino said. "And there are an awful lot of people who will do whatever they can to bring about 'the end times' thinking they can force Jesus to return."

"We've already been debating a bucket list," I said. "But Andy, we can hardly be with you and *not* be aware how little time we might have left, for whatever reason."

Andy looked stricken he might be causing us pain.

"This evening after dinner," I said, "before we watch an episode of *Pushing Daisies*, we're going to make out that list." And it wasn't only about having fun. People wanted to do something useful with their lives, have their lives mean something. "10 Things to Do Before the Apocalypse." We had a small dry erase board on the fridge for our grocery list that could be co-opted.

Santino and I usually left obscene notes for each other. Though it was possible some of those suggestions might make the new list as well.

"And since you're still here," Santino said, "we're going to do some of the things *you* never got around to yet, either."

10 Things to Do Before the Apocalypse

Chapter Six: Andy

The protest was both tiring and uplifting. Lots of people, surprisingly, understood that our leaders and media were lying. Enough video managed to get out of Gaza that the evidence was undeniable.

Except for those who continued to deny.

I began to worry about how ghosts reacted to pepper spray and tear gas.

I supposed Santino and Jake had experienced more criminalization of their existence than I had, being twenty years older. They lived through "AIDS is God's punishment!" and legalized electroshock torture and FBI raids. They lived through the years when even married heterosexual couples practicing oral sex were committing felonies, when gay men caught in the act in their own home could be imprisoned.

Even without their background, I could see what was heading our way.

How long would *our* allies protest?

People's outrage tended to flag over time, like with the Black Lives Matter movement, while the abuses continued unabated.

It was almost enough to make a ghost suicidal.

So after Jake prepared a dinner of sweet potato ziti in carrot bisque soup and veggie meatballs, and an hour of lusting after Lee Pace, the three of us showered and headed to the bedroom. While I was thoroughly enjoying Jake and Santino's company, I couldn't help but wonder if I was accepting the relationship too quickly because I didn't feel I had any other options. Should I go back to the bars and find out if anyone else could see me? Do some "dating" and not jump into a rebound relationship?

Perhaps the three of us felt this instant bonding because we instinctively saw our time together as a summer romance, bound to end all too soon. Of course, every relationship at some level, I supposed, was due to chance and circumstance. I'd never be with Sally Field's gay son because I'd never run into Sally Field's gay son, however well suited we might be.

Since none of those thoughts had an aphrodisiac effect, I kicked them out of my head and focused on body parts.

Like before, we'll try to skip as many sexual details as we can, but that may not be possible altogether when documenting our conversation. So grab a suppository if this stuff gives you a headache.

"How's that ghost sphincter holding out?" Jake asked.

"How's your aging dick holding out?"

"Someone needs a mouthful of mortal cock." Santino straddled my head and thrust himself past my tonsils.

Pro-tip: it's a lot easier to deep throat when you don't need to breathe, even if you're going through the motions. Still, I wouldn't recommend the route I took. I only pushed

Santino's hips back when I could feel his muscles tensing. I didn't want him to overshoot and miss the taste.

I lay with my legs in the air, Jake still pounding away, while savoring Santino's load. I held him in place with his softening dick hanging over me, the occasional drop of cum falling onto my face, while my two lovers kissed one another.

Heaven Can Wait was a great movie, but I didn't have to wait. Sex might not be the pinnacle of either pleasure or happiness, but it was hard to beat this level of intimacy with people you liked. The physical pleasure, as wonderful as it was, paled in comparison to the emotional.

Sandra Bullock's character in *Speed* insisted that relationships that started under intense circumstances never lasted.

But ten years wasn't nothing. Neither was three years. Or three months. A romance didn't need to be eternal to matter.

Almost everyone wanted connection. Almost everyone wanted sex, too. Yet almost everyone seemed to ration both while denying it to others at every opportunity. They punished themselves and others for partaking. They threw up roadblocks. They fought each other, raging with jealousy. And it wasn't as if they were hoarding it for themselves. Almost everyone ended up doing without.

I'd seen videos of flash mobs, with people bursting into song at train stations or in shopping malls, with friends and family surprising their loved ones with proposals in gym classes and on public squares.

The joy and wonder in everyone's eyes was magical.

What would life be like in a world where flash mobs could engage in physical and emotional intimacy? Where such things might be celebrated like dancing to a Bruno Mars or Betty Who song?

Even the one private jack off club I went to before meeting Roland couldn't compare to that.

Jake shot inside me with a final thrust that almost pierced my bladder. He collapsed on top of me, breathing heavily (real breathing). I wrapped my arms tightly around his back.

It was one thing to always know, intellectually, that you might die one day. It was quite another to fear disappearing into the ether at any moment.

When Jake was finally able to move again, he licked the stray drops of cum from my cheeks, leaving one that had fallen onto my beard. I could still smell it.

Heavenly.

"Your turn," Santino said. "How would you like to cum?"

We'd been playing for almost half an hour, only possible with a good deal of edging. I got up on all fours. "I want Jake to kiss me while Santino rims me."

"You can cum like that?"

"I'll stroke myself very slowly. You guys up for a long make out session with both ends?"

I took a short break to clean up in the bathroom before jumping back into bed. Some levels of bliss were simply not attainable without at least three bodies. Because it was easier to control my own orgasm than theirs, I was able to draw out this stage of the evening for another fifteen minutes. I could have held out longer, but I realized they were the ones doing the hard work now.

When I got close, I reared up so I could shoot into my own hand.

[I'm really sorry, guys. Holding back on the sexual details isn't easy when they simply carry so much meaning for us. Hormones being the mind-altering substances they are, these interactions felt downright cosmic. And maybe they're my last attempt at etching "Andy was here!" in the wilderness. So feel free to skim if you must.]

I held out my palm, and Santino scooped my cum into his own hand. Then he pressed it against my asshole and poked some inside me.

"Are you telling me to go fuck myself?" I asked in mock outrage.

"Is it as bad as we've been led to believe?" Santino poked a bit more of the cum sliding down my crack back up into my hole.

"You know, I might never hear that as a slur again."

It wasn't quite 10:00, but we'd all had a long day. We headed to the bathroom to wash our hands but nothing else, wanting to sleep with the remaining sex still everywhere on our bodies. Tonight, Jake lay in the middle, with me spooning up behind him and Santino in front.

The sweat on the back of Jake's neck was intoxicating. He trembled when I rubbed my beard against the back of his head.

I reached across both of them as we fell asleep, calm and nervous at the same time. If I didn't wake up in the morning, at least I was falling asleep content. As content as anyone could really be in a world where joyous flash mobs of any kind were rare.

***

I scrambled some cage-free eggs for breakfast. After all, *I* wasn't worrying about cholesterol. I didn't think it was the right time to explain the problematic nature of free-range and cage-free chicken farms. Time enough for that discussion later.

Well, unless the world ended.

"It's Sunday," Santino said after his first long sip of coffee. "One more day with no obligations before we head back to work. Anyone you want us to question?"

I shook my head. "The first forty-eight hours are the most important in an investigation, and that window closed days ago. We can't talk to anyone at the bank until tomorrow. And I need a break from thinking about death. Let's work on our '10 Things to Do Before the Apocalypse' list."

"Apocalypses *are* relaxing," Santino agreed.

"We're concentrating on the *before* part," I reminded him.

It rather felt like stopping to smell the roses while our necks were being placed in a guillotine, but I supposed it was still better to focus on flowers than the splinters in our necks.

"Catching the ferry to Bainbridge Island's always fun," Jake suggested. "And affordable."

"We need to plan a cruise to see the glaciers in Alaska," I said. "They might not be around much longer."

"And I want to see the Hoh rain forest," Santino declared. "I've lived in Seattle for ages and never been."

"Ooh," I said, "how about paying extra to use the flight simulator at the Museum of Flight?"

We spent the next few minutes brainstorming other possibilities, concentrating on activities reasonably close by. A visit to Multnomah Falls, a trip to Oregon's rocky coast, a hike up at least part of Mount Rainier.

"I suggest we front load these outings," Jake suggested. "If we were planning date nights or even a normal bucket list, one big outing a month might be plenty. But since we don't know how long you'll be here, Andy, and we don't know if we might end up getting arrested as suspects—"

"Or killed by your murderer—"

"—we should probably plan on one outing each weekend."

"Can we have any fun," I asked, "while you guys are being such buzzkills?"

"Hey, I can walk and chew gum at the same time."

"I can fuck and be fucked at the same time," Santino said with a dreamy smile.

"It's all a delicate balance," Jake agreed.

"Everything in moderation." Santino pretended to weigh invisible items in his hands.

"Not *everything*, I hope." I made a rude gesture. While batting my eyes, proving I could multitask, too.

"And we wonder why homophobes think we focus on sex too much."

"No, we wonder why they care whether we think about it or not."

I cleaned up the breakfast dishes, and then we all hopped into the shower. I expected showering separately would soon become the norm, as it did present logistical problems, but for now, we were enjoying getting covered in sex and then washing each other clean again.

I got to put on one of my favorite shirts Santino and Jake had rescued the day before, a T-shirt with a dragon print. If I'd had the nerve while alive, I'd have had a dragon tattooed on my cock. But unless we ran into a ghost tattoo artist, that opportunity had come and gone forever.

I wondered if it was against the law to hire a taxidermist to preserve a tattooed body part after you were dead. It wasn't as if you'd be setting up your stuffed lover in the corner like Roy Rogers did with Trigger. "It's art."

I could just see that argument in front of our current Supreme Court.

The morning was cool but not cold, with low clouds and no drizzle, so Jake and Santino suggested we walk down to the light rail station on Henderson. We passed firs and spruces and redwoods and pines, pink rhododendrons starting to bloom and yards full of blue anemone and white trillium.

We also passed a row of dilapidated RVs along the final stretch, with food wrappers, dirty diapers, and broken glass on the sidewalk. One of the vehicles had a piece of cardboard in the rear window.

A tale of two cities.

At Henderson and MLK, we walked to the middle of the platform, where the monoliths depicting the evolution of horses and several species of dinosaur were posted. Seattle had public art placed in strategic locations across the city. "Paleontologists are always saying how rare the circumstances need to be for fossils to be preserved," I said, fingering an iguanodon. "I can't even keep from breaking a glass or plate for more than a few years."

"The ones Roland's not throwing at you?"

I nodded. "And so many dinosaur fossils have survived not just sixty-five million years but a hundred million, a hundred and thirty million years. Even with erosion and earthquakes and the growth of cities and everything else."

"Yeah?"

"There must have been millions more fossils than we could possibly expect if it was a rare occurrence," I continued. "I wonder…"

"What?" Santino traced the edges of an ankylosaur.

"We see how much more water the atmosphere can hold with even minimal global warming. And it was far hotter during a large portion of the dinosaur era."

"So…?"

I shrugged. "Maybe there were lots of flash floods. Maybe that's why we still have so many fossils even after a hundred million years. That's a *really* long time for this many to have survived."

We all stood looking at the dinosaur monolith a few more moments. "Do you suppose we'll save civilization?" Jake asked. "Before we hit too many tipping points?"

I wondered if our climate had already suffered a mortal wound, if it was bleeding out in a back alley, doomed even if its heart was still beating at the moment.

"I want to know if there are any dinosaur ghosts," I said. "And where human ghosts go when there are no more cities left." I looked at the Polynesian grocery across the street, kitty-corner to a Mexican deli.

I suddenly hoped I *would* dissipate at some point.

Light rail pulled up a few moments later. The cars were mostly empty, so Jake and I sat together while Santino took a place in front of us, turning back to chat.

"You *must* have been killed by a total stranger," Santino said. "No one who knows you could want to hurt you."

"I'm not perfect."

"You don't even know who Tab Hunter is."

"Who?"

"Or Sal Mineo."

"Or Tommy Tune."

"Are those real names?"

"We need to watch some Matt Baume videos on YouTube," Santino decided.

"We have a DVD of *The Celluloid Closet*," Jake added.

Santino tried to pull something up on his phone. "Did you see the campaign ad for that candidate for Secretary of State in Missouri?"

I shook my head.

"The guy took a flamethrower and burned gay library books on camera." He sighed. "Public libraries are getting bomb threats. Vigilantes are showing up with guns at the homes of librarians. Christian conservatives have already filed requests to ban over 4000 books. They…" He stopped with a groan, unable to go on.

And I knew there was plenty more. I vaguely remembered hearing a report about there being something like twenty-five attacks on power substations in the Pacific Northwest over the past few months. I felt like someone working in the World Trade Center at 8:44 a.m. on September 11.

Actually, I felt like the Falling Man, caught forever between life and death.

"Why don't flamethrowers backfire like guns do sometimes?"

Jake nodded toward the other side of the aisle. Santino and I turned to see a teenage Asian girl one row up, staring straight ahead. She'd probably heard everything we said.

Well, two thirds of what we said.

Santino showed us what he'd pulled up on his phone, a meme showing an image of two people talking. The dialogue bubble over the first person enthusiastically cheered, "God sent us Trump!"

The dialogue bubble over the second person countered, "Oh? Did he run out of locusts?"

"Let's add something to our list of things to do," Jake suggested. "Things *not* to do. No news or social media on weekends. The relentlessness is part of the attack."

We thrust our arms up like the Three Musketeers, with Jake saying, "No news is good news!" a little too loudly.

Of course, I didn't really need to worry about being seen with him.

What a privilege it was, I realized, to be embarrassed in public by someone you loved.

We deboarded at the Pioneer Square station and climbed up to street level since neither the elevator nor escalator were working, skirting a pile of human waste on the stairs. Then we headed to the waterfront. Black skid marks from a car that had veered off the road crossed the sidewalk.

The clouds were beginning to break up, but the air was still quite cool. We paid two fares and walked onto the ferry that arrived ten minutes later, finding a place along the railing at the front of the vessel, with the Sound glorious before us.

I stood between Jake and Santino, holding onto their hands. "I don't know if it's possible to feel love this soon," I said, "but it's something very close to it." They each grabbed a hand to squeeze. "If…if I disappear at some point, dissolve or whatever…" I took a ghost breath. "Keep talking to me once in a while as if I was here, just in case."

Chapter Seven: Santino

Anyone who's ever been out on Puget Sound knows it's a glorious experience any time of year. I'd personally never seen an orca, but a pod came through regularly, so quite a few other people had. Last year, there'd been sightings of a humpback whale off Magnolia.

What I loved about ferry rides was the cold breeze slapping against me as the vessel slugged across the water. Even on a hot summer day, the breeze was refreshing. Any other time, it could be quite bracing, as it was today.

That kept most passengers inside on benches or in their cars, but I could sit inside any time I wanted. What I couldn't do often was see the water, feel the salt spray, embrace that cold breeze.

Heaven.

And if this was one of our ten things to do before the apocalypse, I wanted to savor every minute, even if the cold bordered on uncomfortable.

Only as we approached Bainbridge Island did the deck begin to grow crowded. We were in no hurry to be first off, so we stayed up against the railing, even as other passengers scurried about behind us.

"Oof!" I hung onto the railing tightly, almost flipped over by someone in the jostling crowd. Not easy given the railing's height.

"Sheesh! You okay?" Jake grabbed my collar and helped me back to a steady footing.

"Who did that?" Andy demanded. "Did you see?"

We scanned the throng of passengers. No one apologized. No one else even seemed to notice I'd almost gone overboard. "Do you recognize anyone?" I asked Andy.

"You think we were followed?" Jake strained to see over the thinning crowd.

Maybe it was an accident. The coworker who'd sold me mushrooms had been struck by a car while riding his bike to work a couple of years ago. Hit and run. He'd started on psychedelics to deal with his PTSD.

Andy didn't spot anyone he could feel sure about. "That guy," he said, pointing, "could be someone we turned down for a loan, but really, I only saw the customer for a few minutes." He continued searching and then shrugged. "I wouldn't recognize anyone I might have seen at the restaurant my last night, even if they were standing right in front of me now." We looked about for a few more moments, holding fast to the railing.

Had another *ghost* tried to kill me?

Once we docked in Winslow, the passengers quickly deboarded. No one seemed to be looking our way. These days, we could be targeted for being gay. I'd been cursed at once by a Latino who assumed that because I was old and white I must be a MAGA supporter. The dentist I worked for told me she'd removed the mezuzah from her front doorpost not long after Trump was elected in 2016. Said she no longer trusted the community to have her back.

A man whose teeth I was cleaning a few weeks ago told me he wasn't so much afraid of a lone wolf attack or even roving gangs of fundamentalist Christian "patriots." He was afraid of infiltrators in law enforcement and the military. Of judges who supported Q.

"I worry for my non-binary child," he said before I stuck my hand back in his mouth.

As a gay man, it had taken me a long time to understand bisexuality. Even longer to understand transgender folks. I still didn't understand how someone could be non-binary. And the existence of ace folks was an entirely new concept when I first heard about it maybe ten years ago.

I was curious, but I didn't *need* to understand before accepting that people had the right to be who they were.

Jake, Andy, and I decided to remain alert but still relax enough to enjoy our outing. Hardly any point just cowering in a corner, after all. Even here on this idyllic island, though, there were signs of unhappiness.

The forward passenger window of a black Volvo V70 parked under a thick cypress was bashed in, tiny bits of safety glass dotting the seat and floor. Contents from the glove compartment were also scattered across the front seats. An open piece of mail with a cellophane window, an insurance notice, and assorted other papers. Apparently, whoever had broken in was neither fit nor centered and had no intention of becoming so, a cerulean blue yoga mat still rolled up neatly in the back seat, untouched, beside a book encouraging folks to *Live Your Best Life*.

A couple of blocks from shore, we came upon the art museum.

"Buy two admissions," Andy pointed out, "get one free."

"That kind of deal will pay off more if we fly to Japan," I said.

"Or buy tickets on Space X," Jake added.

"Let's go look at pretty paintings." Andy pointed toward the entrance.

The small art museum in Winslow wasn't filled with especially famous works, but the pieces on display were still well worth our time, even if that time was coming to an end, one way or another. There was pottery and sculpture and jewelry and landscapes and abstracts and even a few quilts. Low key and peaceful.

No one who came in after we did seemed to be tracking us. Anyone this good at pretending nonchalance would need to be a professional killer, and surely Andy hadn't warranted that kind of attention.

After a pit stop in the museum bathroom, we continued our excursion with a stroll past the town's many restaurants. "Vegetarian Vietnamese okay?" Jake asked. It was difficult to relax when every decision seemed to carry such weight. Make the day count, I kept telling myself. Make it count.

We bought three entrees, and apparently no one noticed a floating tofu kabob, though Andy ate his across from us at our small table in full view of other patrons. Whatever metaphysical rules were operating, we'd long since given up trying to make sense of them.

"Can you remember anything suspicious in hindsight that anyone did or said your last few days alive?" I asked. The clouds were starting to fill in again, and the breeze even two blocks from the water was cooling off.

Andy shrugged. "Bouchra at work is always making some snide comment," he said. "Last week, she said something snarky about my socks."

Jake raised an eyebrow.

"On Casual Fridays, I wear bright socks—purple or green or red. Maybe dinosaur socks or spaceships or whatever."

"What did she say?" I asked.

"'Your ankles are going to lose us a loan one of these days.'"

Hmm. Perhaps not technically a homophobic slur, but the hint was there. "Did you say anything back?"

Andy shook his head. "I saw Wickens put his hand on his stomach as if he were nauseated. But then, someone else had brought in overly sweet pastries that morning."

"*Can* pastries be too sweet?" I asked. I would always miss them.

"Those two have never liked me," Andy continued, "but that kind of comment was par for the course. Nothing unusual."

"How about at the restaurant?"

"I've wracked my brain and can't think of anything. Petar, the new temp, was talking to Brett and laughed a lot."

"Brett's the gay guy you turned down?"

He nodded. "I don't usually assume people are laughing at me, but it felt like they might be. I don't really know."

Well, this certainly wasn't getting us anywhere.

"Now that I think of it, though," Andy said, "Roland said something just a day or two before that dinner."

"Yeah?"

"He was in the bathroom on his phone as I walked past. I think everyone needs their privacy, even in a committed relationship, so if I accidentally start to overhear something, I try to go somewhere else or turn on the TV. And Roland had only stopped by to pick up a few more things, so we were hardly committed anymore."

"And?"

"He was trying to get a refund for something expensive." Andy shrugged. "He said something like, 'I don't want it anymore.' I heard 'it's too much' and some other comments I can't remember exactly now. Just seemed to be something expensive, whatever it was."

Jake and I looked at each other. "A gift for a boyfriend you don't know about," Jake suggested.

"A deposit on another apartment he wouldn't need because he knew you wouldn't be using the house much longer?" I offered.

"Negotiating the price of a hit man?" Jake added.

"We can fill in an awful lot of blanks with what we *don't* know about that conversation," Andy pointed out.

"Why do you think the refund was for a lot of money?" I asked. "He could have been talking about a $20 item."

Andy shook his head. "Just as I was getting out of range, I heard him say, 'I can't afford to keep…'" He sighed. "I suppose he could have been about to say, 'I can't afford to keep arguing' or 'I can't afford to keep trying to make this relationship work.' Could have been anything, right? I assumed he meant money, but we have separate accounts and I've always felt he could do whatever he wanted with his money. If he helped with the monthly bills, he was free to spend the rest as wisely or as foolishly as he wanted."

Jake and I had our personal accounts, but we also had a joint account for shared bills.

"Anything anyone else said or did come to mind?" I asked.

"I'm afraid I'm a bit self-centered," Andy admitted. "I don't actually pay much attention to what other people say, especially if I don't like them. And that seems to include a lot of people I interact with regularly."

I chuckled. Jake often said the same thing about my attention span.

"I did hear what *you* said about me in your sleep last night." Andy threw a suggestive look Jake's way.

Jake raised an eyebrow again.

"You said, and I quote, 'I want double penetration.'"

"I most certainly did not."

I laughed again. I was the one who sometimes fantasized about it, but Jake didn't even want to be one of the penetrators in such a scenario, much less the penetratee.

"Okay, okay. Maybe *I* was the one mumbling in my sleep." Andy leaned forward with both elbows on the tiny table. "I'm hoping my ghost body doesn't get charley horses, so I can try new positions that'll allow double access."

"How does our murder investigation keep reverting to sex talk?" I asked.

"What would *you* rather think about?" Andy countered. "Having a little fun or being stabbed to death in an alley?"

"I suppose there's a lot to be said for bread and circuses."

We finished our meal, made another pit stop—two of us had prostate issues, after all—and then headed back to the ferry terminal.

Chapter Eight: Santino

Because light rail was sparsely crowded on the trip home, Andy sat in his own seat. But at the Beacon Hill station, a rough looking white guy, heavily tatted, with torn, dirty clothing and bloodshot eyes, spotted us the second he boarded. Even though I was sitting in the aisle seat with Andy next to the window, the guy pushed past me without asking permission, bumping me in the face with a filthy canvas bag, and plopped down right on top of Andy.

Andy disappeared inside the man.

"Um, you okay?" I asked, looking at Jake but hoping Andy could answer.

I assumed the man sitting on top of Andy was homeless or a drug addict or mentally ill or some combination of the three. But perhaps he was employed, housed, and simply rude. I wasn't sure the distinctions mattered as much as the behavior. He turned to me now and said, "What did you do?"

"Excuse me?"

"I feel…I feel…"

"I'm fine." That was Andy. I couldn't see him, but at least he was still here. "I feel weird," he said. "Like I have extra nerve endings."

"Does it hurt?" I asked.

The presumably homeless man shook his head. "I feel good," he told me. "I want whatever you're smoking." He inhaled deeply. "It must still be in the air." He breathed in again.

"I don't hurt," Andy said, "but I feel sick. Let's move."

We stood and hurried down the aisle and into the next car. "You okay?" I asked again once we found another empty spot.

Andy nodded. "That wasn't pleasant," he said. "But it wasn't *entirely* unpleasant, either." He paused. "Someday, I might want to try that under more favorable circumstances."

"Andy," Jake said, "you can get inside me any way you want, any time you want."

"Are we writing greeting cards?" I asked.

Andy snorted, clearly feeling better already. "You sure know how to win a ghost's heart."

"But you won't be able to merge with us, will you?" I realized. "You're tangible to us."

"And it wouldn't be ethical to merge with someone you guys randomly pick up at the bar." Andy's brows furrowed.

"Maybe sometime, we'll ask one of our fuck buddies," Jake said. "But that will require a conversation I'm not ready for yet."

Back at the house, all I wanted to do was take a nap, emotionally beat. Just as I was about to suggest a brief spooning session, my cell phone pinged.

"It's Tyler," I said, reading the message.

Andy gave me a questioning look.

"We see our friend Tyler on Sundays once or twice a month," Jake said.

"You guys play?" Andy asked.

"Once in a while," I said. "We started out platonic ten years ago but then started playing a few years later." I realized that sexual intimacy usually worked in the other direction, but there were so many factors involved—including the relationship status of the other individual—that these things were often unpredictable. I could feel strongly attracted to a man for years and never make a move if I felt it would be inappropriate for that relationship.

But when Tyler ended a relationship with a guy we'd never particularly liked and announced, "I need some break up sex," Jake and I were happy to accommodate. We now played together a few times a year but mostly getting together to chat about his work or watch a movie.

"Want to come along?" I asked.

"You weren't really going to leave me behind, were you?"

"You've still got autonomy. Maybe you'd rather listen to music or read a book."

Andy shook his head.

"It's okay to want down time."

He shook his head again, and I smiled. I wasn't ready for a break yet, either.

My phone pinged. "He's preempting sex," I said. "Wants to talk." Tyler was good about letting us know what he did and didn't want. It was amazing how many people were afraid to do that, adding unnecessary awkwardness to what should be normal, pressure-free interactions.

Tyler lived on Beacon Hill. Jake, Andy, and I walked down Renton to Fifty-first and waited for the 107, arriving at our friend's place twenty minutes later.

It was difficult to cultivate friendships with guys who lived much farther away.

Was it selfish to be grateful Andy had nowhere else to go?

Yes. Yes, it was. And I was grateful.

Tyler welcomed us both with a kiss.

"You have the most wonderful tongue," I said. Tyler always gave us deep kisses, even when no play was on the agenda. With some guys, a peck was plenty, but I liked Tyler's tongue.

Jake liked his ears.

"What's that on his skin?" Andy asked.

I ignored him. One couldn't just speak randomly into the air about someone's psoriasis, after all.

Tyler had coffee brewing and poured us each a cup. We sat in his kitchen while he told us his latest work troubles.

"The card readers were down for two days. My work email won't load. My coworkers spend time on the computer shopping. They text their friends instead of waiting on customers. And I can't really say anything to them or to my supervisor without looking like a jerk."

"We're happy to offer venting opportunities," Jake said.

"Only fifteen more years until retirement age."

Jake and I groaned at the same time. The latest notice I'd received from Social Security informed me that if I retired this year at the age of sixty-three, I'd get $1231 a month. If I waited until I was sixty-seven, I'd get $1785. If I waited until I reached the age of seventy, I'd get $2200 a month. Even that wouldn't be enough to live on. Not in Seattle, anyway.

Jake's monthly check would be even less, but together, we could survive. We simply wouldn't be retiring anytime soon.

There was a certain bleakness to a future of unending work at an unfulfilling job, stealing away our last remaining good hours of life, hoping we weren't incapacitated by a stroke first. One way or another, though, we'd be working until we dropped dead.

But Tyler certainly didn't need to hear that today.

"Want us to sign up as Secret Shoppers and report on your coworkers?" I asked.

Tyler laughed. "Wouldn't mind a couple of Yelp reviews naming names, but I don't want to be as big a jerk as they are."

"I sense a lot of self-jerk avoidance."

"Did you have to talk about self jerking?" Andy asked.

We chatted a bit more about other things going on in Tyler's life, and then he asked for updates about ours. Of course, we couldn't include every detail, but we did catch him up about Andy's murder, describing him as a new acquaintance.

"Do you know if this guy had any beneficiaries besides his husband?" Tyler asked.

Jake rubbed the back of his head as if trying to remember, glancing over at Andy, who in turn frowned and rubbed his chin. "I did make my gay nephew Ryan the beneficiary for a single CD. Just over $10,000."

Jake passed the information on to Tyler.

"Does the nephew know about it?" Tyler asked.

Andy nodded, so I said, "Yes."

"Is the nephew in financial trouble?"

Andy frowned again and turned away, so I shrugged. We chatted about a few other things, and then it was almost time to go.

"Why don't you put on some soothing music," I suggested, "and lie down. Jake and I will give you a back massage until you drift off, and then we'll let ourselves out."

We headed into Tyler's bedroom, waiting as he pulled up Hidden Citizens. He stripped to his underwear and lay face down as the lyrics to "Immortalized" began drifting hauntingly from the speakers.

The items on our list of things to do before the apocalypse were necessarily specific. Otherwise, it would be too hard to make sure we'd done them. But it seemed clear that more important than any one action was to make sure we took care of each other at every possible moment.

We gently rubbed our friend's back for the next twenty minutes, until his steady breathing let us know he'd fallen asleep for a late afternoon nap. Then we quietly let ourselves out.

Chapter Nine: Jake

"You want to go to your nephew's apartment," Santino asked, "and look around? Watch him for a while?"

We were walking back up the hill after stepping off the 107. On Sundays it was faster to walk the last half mile than wait for a transfer. And it wasn't as if we didn't need the exercise of a steep climb.

Andy shook his head. "If it was Ryan, I'd rather not know," he said. "If that means my soul won't rest and I'm forced to stick around, I'm okay with that."

"We want you around, too," I said. "And we want you to *also* be at peace."

We walked underneath the low hanging branches of a spruce. "I've been hoping to narrow down the list of suspects," Andy said, "not expand it."

I supposed there'd always be things we'd never know. If there was any collusion in the JFK assassination. What happened to D.B. Cooper. If Ronald Reagan liked to be pegged by Nancy.

Well, I expected we knew the answer to that last question.

We strolled past a raised planter of strawberries. Blooms but no berries yet. A yard full of purple azaleas. A snowball bush, with its round clusters of white flowers. Another yard bordered with bunchberry in bloom, like dogwood as groundcover.

And then passed a few campers and RVs. A man sat in a lawn chair beside one, reading a tattered paperback. We stepped into the street when the sidewalk a bit further along was obstructed by blackberry briars.

The mystery we really couldn't answer was "what happens next?" The fact that Andy was here *might* mean there was "life" after death, but it could also simply be a brief stage right before complete and final dissolution, like the Wicked Witch of the West melting after being splashed with a bucket of water. Santino believed that near-death experiences proved we continued after our bodies died. But many researchers believed they only showed a specific type of brain activity under severe stress. The scientific method wasn't equipped to answer a question that required the kind of evidence a physical body could never provide.

If there truly were a god, though, why wouldn't ghosts be haunting murderers rather than hanging out with new pals? Especially mass murderers like presidents and prime ministers and other government officials who signed the papers authorizing those murders.

"Have you seen any other ghosts?" I asked.

Andy shook his head again. "No one's looked me in the eyes and made contact. There's been no moment of recognition or anything."

"Wouldn't it be great…" I brushed my fingers along the waxy, blue-green needles of another spruce. "…if ghosts could organize and form a union, protest in front of the homes of senators and members of Congress who pass bills that cut medical aid or food for children?"

Or haunt hateful school board members, like those in Virginia who voted to restore the names of Confederate leaders to their schools. A lone member voted against the action. I'd sent him an email thanking him for his courage. It shouldn't take courage to vote against honoring traitors, but these days, unfortunately, it did.

Santino laughed.

Andy didn't. "If that could be done, wouldn't some other ghost have thought of it by now?"

"If there's one ghost," I pressed, "there must be others."

Santino put his fist to his chin and bowed his head, striking a pose not unlike that of Rodin's Thinker.

"Maybe we're like ships that pass in the night," Andy said. "Like trees that fall in the forest when no one's there to hear."

"Well, who the hell made up *that* metaphysical rule?"

Andy reached out and pulled us to a stop underneath the low branches of a redwood beside a bus stop. "I'm scared about leaving and not scared. I mean, maybe I'll see my mom and grandma again. Maybe I won't. And maybe I'll never see you again." He pulled me close and gave me a kiss.

"Schroedinger's afterlife?" Santino asked.

"We'd better do what we can for you while you're here," I said. "Make some calls to your friends and family who you want to hear a final message. Tell them you left it with us to pass on when the time came, that you didn't trust Roland to do it."

Andy nodded. "You guys should probably call *your* friends and family, too, and tell them you love them. While you still can." He peered up from underneath the branches. "Another Boeing door plug might fall from the sky."

***

It was still a bit early for another meal, and after so much philosophizing, I suggested we do something to relax. That was *supposed* to be what the ferry ride was for. "Who's up for a game of Scrabble?"

"I-A-M," Santino replied.

"That's two words," Andy pointed out.

I set up the board while Andy grabbed a few cans of lemon seltzer water. Santino and I liked making new rules on occasion. Perhaps we'd allow names of countries or cities. A couple of times, we tried to only place words in languages other than English on the board.

"Tonight," I said, "how about we only write proper names? Men we've loved throughout our lives." I thought about Willie Nelson's "To All the Girls I've Loved Before."

Then I thought about his duet with Orville Peck. "Cowboys are Secretly Frequently Fond of Each Other."

"We better include names of men we merely like as well," Santino suggested.

"Or have at least slept with," Andy amended.

"All right, all right," I said. "And the names of guys we *wish* we'd slept with, too."

***

While Santino packed away the board and tiles later, I cooked dinner, green beans from the freezer, with Miyoko cashew butter and a dash of pepper, alongside sliced eggplant sprinkled with my own secret combination of spices. "That recipe will go with me to the grave," I declared.

Andy put his hands on his hips.

Afterward, we sent emails to three of Andy's friends, to a cousin, to a former coworker, and then made calls to his brother and his brother's son Ryan, the latest possible suspect. The emails were easy enough. Andy could pull up his contact list on our computer, so he didn't even need to remember the addresses. But the phone calls, those required we prepare an outline with bullet points to sound convincing.

Neither family member questioned our association with Andy. The calls went smoothly, and Ryan didn't say anything that sounded suspicious.

"I should have left some money to a black organization," Andy said when we'd finished, "or a Native American group. Made some tiny effort at reparations that our government never will. Intergenerational wealth is a real thing, and I missed my chance to help with that one."

Santino glanced at me, and I knew we'd have a serious conversation in the coming days on the subject. In the day to day grind, it was easy to postpone heavy topics, both out loud and internally, but spending so much time with a dead man forced a lot of this to the surface.

And the constant onslaught of worrisome news was making it difficult to avoid "deep thoughts" even on my most "ignorance is bliss" days.

I smiled, remembering Jack Handey's spots on *Saturday Night Live*.

Avoidance. Again.

But there comes a moment when your own mortality becomes more than theoretical.

In Louisiana, a bill was making its way through the state legislature to label abortion pills "controlled substances" and sentence anyone with such medication in their possession to five years in prison. In Texas, the GOP wanted to execute anyone who had an abortion.

I pulled out a large mixing bowl and started peeling some bananas. "Could you hand me the potato masher, please?" Andy rummaged in a drawer and handed it to me.

Did his existence make the prospect of being murdered after the election less terrifying?

I began smashing the potatoes vigorously. I supposed Andy had a point. We were all part of an economic ecosystem. Like a tree falling in the forest and providing nutrients for the next generation of growth, we could offer sustenance for the equivalent of endangered economic species.

Mutual aid as an act of defiance. Rewriting Dylan Thomas's poem to read, "Rage, rage, against the dying of democracy."

I reached into a cabinet and pulled out a jar of tahini paste, like peanut butter but made from sesame seeds. No sugar, no added palm oil or anything else. Just crushed seeds made into paste. I scooped out several large spoonfuls and added them to the bananas. Baking was a useful kind of avoidance, I hoped. All-natural ingredients were good for the gut, whatever they did to our waistline.

"It's counterintuitive, isn't it?" Santino asked. "We want people to mourn us, miss us, be sad we're gone, but we want to leave something positive behind so our death will benefit them, too." He handed me a package of walnut pieces.

I scooped out half a cup, breaking the larger pieces into smaller ones and adding them to the bowl. I thought about how a single walnut required five gallons of water to produce. Then I thought about how much fuel it took to ship food overseas or even between states. I remembered reading that it was cheaper for some companies to manufacture part of a product in one country, ship it to another for the next part of the manufacturing process, and then ship it back.

"We'll never be rich enough to make much of a difference with our wills," I said. I threw in a spoonful of crushed flax seeds and crushed chia seeds, then squeezed some raw honey into the mixture.

"We could leave our house to an organization that helps rescue trafficked women," Santino suggested.

"I wish…" Andy began. "I wish…" His voice trailed off.

These were never going to be fun conversations.

While the oven was preheating, I added a few cups of oats into the mixing bowl and stirred the thick mess until my arm grew tired.

Seattle had a handful of community gardens throughout the city but not nearly enough. Yet we were still one of the better places in the U.S. for outdoor spaces, with over ten percent of the city reserved for public parks.

"Don't forget the protein." Santino handed me some vegan peanut butter protein powder, and I added two scoops to the mixture.

I was too tired to make a quip about extra protein. "We'd better try harder to make a contribution to society while we're still alive," I said. "I don't think we can count on what happens after we're gone."

"I donated $500 once to help make a documentary on the passenger pigeon," Andy said with a shrug.

I'd been thinking about near-death experiences earlier, and what was it that most people telling these stories kept saying was the most important thing they realized they needed to be doing with their lives?

Making and maintaining loving relationships.

While the cookies were baking, I wrote a longish email to Craig, our friend with cancer, while Santino chatted on the phone with our straight friend Osman. He was a former neighbor, German Turkish, who'd since moved to Shoreline, so we didn't see him as much. When we did, he liked to watch shows like *Homicide: Istanbul* with us, pointing out every time the subtitles were wrong.

In the mood now for European television, I suggested we watch an episode of *Inspector Ricciardi* while we snuggled on the sofa, with the actor who played a ghost in *La Porta Rossa* now playing a detective in fascist Napoli of the 1930s who could see the ghosts of people who were brutally murdered, hear their last thoughts before dying.

We each ate a fresh cookie while we watched.

After the show came the worst part of every weekend, preparing for bed and knowing that once we fell asleep, we'd wake up to another week with little time to enjoy our lives. Thomas Edison was reported to have said he never worked a day in his life, that it was all fun. The implication was that if we didn't feel the same way about our jobs, we had bad attitudes and therefore deserved any unhappiness we experienced in the workplace.

Funny how that kind of judgment so often seemed to come from those who benefitted from the work of others, taking the profit for themselves.

"I'm not really in the mood for sex tonight," Santino said as we climbed into bed. "You guys okay with just kissing for a while?"

It was difficult to roll around on top of each other kissing for thirty minutes without becoming aroused, but Santino and I weren't the type who needed to conclude every erection with an orgasm. Andy didn't insist, either. He finally fell asleep between us, one arm across Santino's chest, his face in Santino's armpit. I rested my head against Andy's back, one leg thrown across his, while I drifted off to sleep as well.

***

No sex the next morning, either. We were quickly becoming an old married throuple.

But there was a fascinating story in the *New York Times* about a polyamorous group of seven or eight people, the differing primary couplings in the group, the shifts, the insecurities, and the strengths.

Perhaps if we ran into any more ghosts…

"Almost two hundred bodies found in a mass grave at a hospital in Gaza," Santino said as we sipped coffee.

I groaned.

"Elderly, children, patients with catheters still in place. Bodies with their hands tied behind their backs."

We listened to more news while Andy cooked a quick breakfast. Librarians in Louisiana could face two years with hard labor for paying dues to their professional association. A bill was advancing in Alabama that would make offering "gender-oriented" material to minors a criminal offense.

"Like books with male characters?" Santino asked. "Or female characters?"

"How about books with animals?" I added. "They're gendered, too."

Andy gasped. "What about dinosaurs?" His face darkened with a frown. "*They* have genders!"

"So do some plants," Santino pointed out. "No books about them, either?"

"For God's sake," Andy interrupted, setting an omelet made with cashew cheese in front of us, "do you guys start off every Monday with *that* kind of pep talk?"

I shrugged. "I don't want to head off to work not knowing if there's been another coup."

"Can't we focus on positive news?" he pressed. "I heard a few weeks ago that Greece legalized same-sex marriage." He started preparing an omelet for himself. "Some governor—was it in Connecticut?—used a grant to pay off the medical debt for some of his state's residents." He wrinkled his nose, trying to come up with another bit of happy news.

"I did hear last week that the European Court of Human Rights ruled that not taking enough action to tackle climate change is a violation of human rights." It was unlikely such a ruling would have a practical impact, but just as every degree of warming mattered, so did every act of resistance.

"Let's add positive energy to the world," Andy said. He flipped his omelet. "Kind of like amplifying the voices of the marginalized. Let's amplify the underrepresented positive energy out there."

"I can see why Roland loved you."

"He didn't love me. He was obsessed with me." He chuckled. "But that's a negative thought. Let's refocus. What are you guys doing today?"

Santino would be heading to a dental office in Columbia City where he worked as a hygienist. I'd be heading to a home improvement store in Renton where I worked in an office ordering supplies and doing other paperwork so boring it was never a topic of conversation at home.

"And you?" I asked. "Did you want to hang out with either of us or just stay here and watch some TV?"

Andy slid his omelet onto a plate and sat at the table to start eating. "I'll be shadowing suspects," he said. "Going to the bank to eavesdrop. And heading to Pioneer Square to see if I can catch any tips from homeless folks there." He took a bite of his omelet, his eyes closing as he savored the experience. "Someone," he said, "knows something. And I'm going to find out who killed me." He paused dramatically and stabbed another bite of egg. "Even if it kills me."

Chapter Ten: Andy

I was a little frightened to watch Santino and Jake head off to work. What if I ceased to exist while they were gone? Worse, what if I *didn't* cease to exist, but they were no longer able to see me after we'd been separated for hours? I could be on my knees, begging and pleading, and...nothing.

They'd think I abandoned them.

But there was nothing I could do about it, so I walked down to the light rail station and caught the train to Pioneer Square. At least I didn't have to worry about fare ambassadors.

Pioneer Square isn't a public square, and the area isn't even visible when you exit the Pioneer Square station. The neighborhood is between that station and the Chinatown/International District station, probably closer to the latter but not exactly there, either. It's over a few blocks toward the water, several minutes away from either stop.

The oldest part of the city, Pioneer Square was a rough neighborhood even before the pandemic. Months of low tourism and locals afraid to congregate had led to many restaurants and other longstanding businesses folding. Even as life picked up again, the area struggled. A few Christian charities offered assistance to the destitute, but as most of those operating here were blatantly homophobic, I never donated to them.

I passed a couple of alleys like the one where I'd been murdered. Nothing in them but large metal garbage bins. Once I reached Second Avenue, I headed to the restaurant where I'd last eaten with my coworkers.

But what was I going to do now? The place wasn't even open at this hour. I stood beside the front door and studied the people walking by.

No girl from Ipanema.

No murderer, either, as far as I could tell. No eyes locked onto mine, giving the culprit away.

An hour later, I was slapping myself in the face to stay awake, stretching and awkwardly trying to massage my lower back.

When a homeless woman in her thirties trudged by, I decided to follow. Perhaps she'd talk to other folks on the street. The 24-hour news cycle was probably a reality in this world, too. Any murders, especially if not one of their own, had probably long since evaporated as a topic of conversation.

But it wasn't as if I had lots of alternatives.

Belinda, it turned out, headed to a non-profit past First Avenue, where she picked up her mail. I hung out in the building for a while, watching other unhoused folks do laundry, pick up checks, and take showers, eavesdropping on several conversations.

Promyse liked to argue about everything.

Baraka was battling addiction. Not very successfully.

Steve was only allowed to withdraw small amounts of money at a time so he wouldn't spend it all on alcohol in two days.

Justin kept talking to people who weren't there. Given the circumstances, I wasn't sure if he was schizophrenic or seeing other ghosts that I couldn't. I called out, asking them to pass a message to Justin, but if they were real, they didn't seem able to see or hear me, either.

I finally tired of the place and followed Justin out of the building and down the street. We stepped over an unconscious man in a sleeping bag, using a roll of paper towels still covered in plastic as a pillow. We passed a law office, a deli, a couple of boarded up shops, a toy store—really?—and the offices for Underground Seattle.

I'd done the tour years ago, but it was something else to add to our list of things to do before the apocalypse. Both fun and interesting. I glanced down at the purple glass bricks in the sidewalk that allowed light to enter what used to be ground level in the 1800s.

One block farther, Justin ran into another man, perhaps forty, not much older than him. "'Sup, Mattie?" He waved weakly.

Mattie shrugged and motioned with his shoulder for Justin to follow. The two continued walking down the street, with me trying to stay close enough to overhear their dialogue. I wasn't a fly. I couldn't get right up next to their faces. While they couldn't see or feel me, I felt everything and everyone I bumped into. So I had to follow behind, not beside the two men, and as their voices were projected forward, I could barely make out the gist of their conversation.

It didn't seem to matter. I picked up a few words about bread, I think, something about the Mariners, and comments about the weather. But nothing about murder.

Hardly a surprise. With hundreds of homeless folks in the area, the chances I'd tail the one or two people who might know what happened were pretty slim, even after a few hours of loitering.

The two men walked past Second, along the edge of the block where the restaurant was located. And then it happened. Justin paused at the alley that led behind the businesses. He pointed into the alley. "I saw what happened here."

Mattie clapped Justin on the back and they kept walking.

You know those dreams where you're running but you feel like you're in quicksand? Or those times you're in that stage of sleep called sleep paralysis? I tried putting my hands on Justin's shoulder to stop him, tried shouting, clapping, kicking a piece of trash into his path. But he couldn't hear me to answer my questions. Did Justin see the murder as it happened? See me after the fact?

Why wasn't Mattie asking these questions? Was that because he knew another unhoused person was responsible? Or because an unhoused person *wasn't* responsible?

I tried jumping into Justin's body, but whatever he had going on inside wasn't pleasant, and I jumped right back out. He didn't even seem to notice.

"Frustrating" was too long a word for Wordle. Even for Scrabble.

Was "Aaaahhh" a word? Seven letters.

While there was still no evidence one way or the other that a homeless person was responsible, I realized I didn't *want* to believe my death was random. Better to be targeted for almost any ideological reason, even jealousy, than to matter so little that killing me was like squashing a bug.

But if it was some guy acting out, like that mentally ill man at the Capitol Hill light rail station who'd stabbed a fellow for brushing past him on the escalator, I'd need to leave the investigation up to the police. Of course, if I couldn't find the killer with all my spare time and no possibility of being noticed by the suspects, it was unlikely the detectives would fare much better.

Really, it was surprising many murders were solved at all.

I pulled out my cell phone and dialed. A moment later, Jake answered. "You okay?" he asked.

"I discovered something."

"The murderer?"

I sighed. "I learned I like puzzles. But only simple ones."

"You sure you're okay?"

I briefly summarized my activities of the morning.

"And…so you're heading back to the toy store?" Jake asked. "I'm not quite following."

"I always did like jigsaw puzzles," I explained, "but only the 500-piece and maybe 750-piece ones, never anything harder. I liked Organic Chemistry in college, but only enough to minor in it, not major." I sighed again, mostly relieved to find I could still talk to Jake. That hadn't been a given.

"I'm sorry it's been frustrating for you," he said.

"I'll try one more thing," I told him. "And then I'll head home and wait for you guys."

Now it was Jake's turn to sigh. "I'm glad you're calling our place home," he said. "It *is* your home, too."

"Maybe if you hand me a key personally, it'll work if I use it by myself."

"I'm sorry we didn't even think to try."

"See you tonight, sweetie." Roland hated terms of endearment. It felt great to use one now. And mean it.

I was only a few blocks away now from the bank where I worked. Even that short distance meant moving into another world. Still some tents on the sidewalks in front of boarded up businesses but also lots more high rises, forty, sixty, seventy stories tall. People who needed banking services regularly.

I passed the tellers and the folks on the platform selling car loans and credit cards, moving to a side room where the mortgage crew lived. There was Marilyn. Bouchra, too. Brett and Petar. Plus, boring Wickens. And the rest.

Here on Gilligan's Isle.

[I did not write that. I've heard of the show but never seen it. And I'm not culturally illiterate, so I think if that was a joke, it flopped. But I apparently don't have the final say in these things.]

I wanted to type "Who's the murderer?" on someone's computer. [This part is really me.] Maybe piss in Wickens's coffee. [Yep, still me.] I remembered the subway scene from the movie *Ghost*. Apparently, ghosts could be mentally ill, too.

I wished I could push a penny.

My desk still had all my stuff on it. Mostly neat but not perfect. I felt oddly touched that no one had straightened things up. It still looked as if I might return at any moment. I pulled out the chair and sat, looking about at my coworkers, all energetically working away. Well, energetically pretending to work.

Life goes on, right?

I hung around for another half hour, and another. If the job was boring to do, it was far worse observing. Then lunch time came around, always staggered, of course. I watched as Wickens and Petar, the new guy, headed for the break room in back. Petar had only brought a sandwich, but I could see him taking his time at the counter until Wickens sat down, and then sitting on the far side of the room away from him.

Perhaps it was good they couldn't hear me chuckle.

"Petar," Wickens said, gathering his things and moving closer to Petar, "I know you're not interested in baseball."

Petar closed his eyes and took a breath.

"You've always been so patient with me when I talk about it because you know I like baseball. I can talk about baseball pretty much every day during baseball season. I know I talk about it too much, and you're so patient."

Petar forced a smile, an odd look when combined with gritted teeth.

"You know I follow the Mariners religiously. That I really enjoy them. But I doubt you watched the game this weekend. And I don't know if anyone else has talked to you about the game. I don't know if you have friends or neighbors who have talked about it. Maybe a brother or father who called you. I don't know if you heard anything on the news."

Had I stabbed *myself* in that alley?

"You may have, of course, but I don't know."

Petar stuffed the sandwich into his mouth, taking a huge bite, whether to keep himself from screaming or to finish as quickly as possible, I couldn't tell.

"So I don't know if you know the highlights of the event, or what I think were the highlights. But there were two things during the game this weekend that were really meaningful to me, and because you're so patient and know it's important to me, I'm going to tell you what those two things were."

Why had I not looked harder for another job? Most of us spent the majority of our waking lives in the workplace. Why deliberately allow so much of our lives to feel like this?

"I'll just mention the two things because I don't want to take up too much of your time, when you're being so generous and patient with me. I could mention more than two things. I could go on and on because I really like baseball, but I'll keep this short. Unless you'd like to hear more."

I discovered that ghosts can walk right out of a room without offending anyone, so I did.

Chapter Eleven: Santino

My phone pinged just as I was polishing Mr. Hernandez's teeth. After I offered him a wooden toothbrush and encouraged him yet again to consider flossing between visits—"just between those teeth you want to keep"—I directed him to the reception area to make his next appointment.

Then I checked my phone. Andy had texted, "Can you talk?" and I felt a thrill. That early stage of infatuation was lovely. And I couldn't help feeling oddly superior to "normal" people. How many folks, after all, got texts from ghosts? But then I worried it might be bad news. It was time for my break anyway, so I popped outside behind our clinic and called. "You okay?"

"I miss you!" Andy shouted. He fake wailed like a child.

I chuckled. I missed him, too. And Jake. I always missed Jake when we weren't together. We'd given each other our personal space from the start, and that worked for us, but it didn't mean we didn't enjoy being together, too.

Andy caught me up on his adventures shadowing homeless folks and his coworkers at the bank. Made cleaning tartar and plaque sound exciting.

"But I did finally learn how to push a penny," he said.

"Excuse me?"

"The only thing I've managed to do that people besides you and Jake can see is to pull up songs on a music streaming service."

"Really?" There was no point trying to make sense of it. Perhaps it was just the start of developing more useful abilities. Like mastering Candy Crush.

"I'm afraid I'm being a bit of a dick," Andy admitted. "I know Bouchra hates country music so I'm playing Beyoncé on the computer in her office. Whenever she closes the tab, I open it again."

I snorted.

"And Wickens only listens to gospel, so I keep playing David Archuleta at his desk."

"A bit passive aggressive, are we?" I asked.

"It passes the time and gives me some practice."

"You trying to advance from ghost to poltergeist?"

"Is that like moving from Tenderfoot to Second Class?"

An idea suddenly popped into my mind. "Do your coworkers know your favorite song? Or your favorite band?"

There was a pause as Andy reflected. "Probably. Why?"

"Play that and see who reacts."

"Do some actual haunting?"

"See if anyone looks guilty."

There was another pause. "I suppose that's a *bit* less dickish anyway," Andy said. "But in my defense, I did hear Bouchra and Wickens talking in her office. He made some comment about hoping she hired someone with a better moral character to replace me, and she admitted she'd wanted to get rid of me for a long time but that I was protected by law."

"Sheesh, and you didn't lead with that news?"

"I also discovered that while eavesdropping is great, detectives have one advantage I don't."

"What's that?"

"They can ask questions."

"And hear lies in response," I said.

"I suppose I could hang out with some of my coworkers at their homes and snoop, but no one here's especially high on my suspect list anyway."

"Really? Because those two sound highly sus to me."

"Maybe. But if I go home with them, that's two evenings I'll lose with you."

"Isn't finding your killer worth two evenings? Jake and I can stay up late and give you a warm welcome when you get in."

Andy sighed. "What are the chances a murderer will leave evidence lying around to implicate themselves? I can't see them writing about such a thing in their journal or chatting about it with their friends." He paused. "I'd rather spend my evenings with you guys. I still don't know how long I'm going to be here."

Or how long *we* might be here, I thought. Wildfires in Chile had killed more than 130 people. Dubai had received a year and a half of rain in one day. Howler monkeys were dropping dead out of trees in Mexico because of the heat. Over 140 people had been murdered by ISIS in an attack on a concert hall in Moscow.

Nothing in life was sure in the best of times.

Stopping off at the store on the way home wasn't a trivial matter when you were on public transit, but we needed more banana oatmeal walnut butter flax seed protein powder cookies for dessert tonight. If I bought the ingredients Jake wanted, he'd cook.

"Monoculture is as bad for food as it is for society," he'd told me after reading up more on the subject a couple of years earlier. "We need more DEI in our beets and carrots and squash." No more foods with high fructose corn syrup or palm oil. No more food with added sugars.

That eliminated lots of options. There were certain foods we simply couldn't eat anymore or at least only rarely. Balancing healthier eating with our refusal to be fanatics.

Another way to feel excluded from mainstream society.

Coming home to Jake almost always felt like entering a sanctuary. Like any couple, we had our bad moments. There seemed nothing worse than to be out in the "cold, cruel world" all day and then come home to stress and animosity. So we did our best to work through our problems quickly.

Jake's mother had framed a cross stitch quote for us that read, "Do you want to be right or do you want to be happy?" The power behind that was in offering both of us a moral out to go ahead and give in and apologize when we had conflicts.

My mom had risen to the competition and learned cross stitch as well, so she could gift us with another framed quote, this one from Ogden Nash: "To keep your marriage brimming, with love in the loving cup, whenever you're wrong, admit it. Whenever you're right, shut up."

Both our mothers were dead now.

You never really stopped missing some people.

"Santino!" Andy rushed off the porch to greet me, taking the bags out of my hands and hugging me tightly.

"I love you, too."

Despite running an errand on my way back, I still beat Jake home. He arrived just as Andy and I finished preparing dinner. Veggie burgers with spicy green beans and fried carrot sticks. Purple carrot sticks.

He handed Andy a Sudoku book.

"Intermediate level," Andy noted with a smile.

I'd clearly missed something, but I felt a little thrill knowing the two of them already had private conversations. The three of us were still individuals, after all. We couldn't do or think everything as a unit.

[Now *I'm* throwing in an edit, Mr. Let's-try-to-make-our-voices-uniform-in-this-account. How do you spell the sound of blowing a raspberry?]

As we sat down to eat, we reviewed Andy's activities of the day once more, hoping to catch something we'd missed before. But nothing stood out. Other than the reality that Andy really was dead. Even if his ghost managed to stick around, his life, his existence, was permanently altered. Like a skier surviving a crash with a spinal cord injury.

While a skier might be able to cope with that change through therapy and a good support group, it would surely be more difficult if he or she knew someone had caused that crash intentionally.

"I always hate when we watch detective shows," Jake said, "and at some point when one character or another is seeking revenge, someone else will say, 'But that won't bring so-and-so back, will it?'"

"You want revenge?" Andy asked. I couldn't tell if he was touched or concerned by the thought.

"Isn't the same thing true of justice?" Jake pressed. "Justice won't bring anyone back to life, either. Neither will ignoring the crime. Nothing will. So do we just do nothing?"

Andy nodded. "I've been wondering if it even matters who killed me. I mean, I'm curious. I want to know. But what then?" He shrugged. "If he isn't arrested or convicted, do I just Spotify the creep to death?"

I remembered a news story from decades earlier, about a man who broke into his neighbor's apartment and threw the guy's stereo out the window into the street below after the neighbor kept playing Whitney Houston's cover of "I Will Always Love You" on a loop.

Jake bit off the end of a crunchy fried carrot. "But then I wonder how much a single death, even someone as important to us as you, matters in the bigger scheme."

Andy frowned.

"What good is it to find someone who murdered one person when fascists might take over and kill thousands?" Jake said. "Wouldn't our time be better spent phone banking to prevent that? Going to rallies? Raising money for the ACLU? Maybe for All Out to help rescue LGBTQ folks from even more homophobic countries?"

I snorted. "As long as we don't bring them here," I said.

"You don't like immigrants?" Andy's eyes widened.

"I don't want to put them in an 'out of the frying pan, into the fire' situation. Like a gay *Voyage of the Damned*."

Andy caught the reference. "Delaying brutality is still better than allowing it to go unchecked."

"And we're back to the problem of doing nothing." Jake bit into another crunchy fried carrot. "There's never going to be a permanent solution. It'll always be a battle to maintain rights and protect people."

"And protect the environment. You can't uncut down old growth trees."

"I suppose," I said, "the point of catching Andy's murderer is to make sure the murderer doesn't kill again."

"Not justice *or* revenge." Andy nodded. "Just protecting people who will never know they were in danger to begin with."

"Like students where a school shooting never happened because it was caught in time."

Andy nodded again. "Then we'll keep looking."

We watched an episode of *Dead Boy Detectives* after dinner, with me lying across Jake's and Andy's laps on the sofa. "At least we don't have to deal with a whole supernatural world of evil like these guys," I said.

"Would that be worse than the real-world evil we *do* have to deal with?" Andy asked.

"I didn't want to say anything," Jake said, "but I heard another unpleasant story on the news."

"Who are you kidding?" Andy snorted. "You'd have an aneurysm if you tried to stop yourself from 'sharing' these awful stories."

"I do keep imagining the worse," he admitted, "but it's possible that if fascists take over in November, we *won't* all be rounded up or killed. We might only get castrated."

I swallowed wrong and choked on my spit. "Wh-what? Did you say 'only'?"

Jake shrugged. "A bill's progressing through the legislature in Louisiana," he said, "to force child molesters to be surgically castrated."

Everyone was silent for a long moment. Finally, Andy said, "I'm not sure that's a bad idea."

"That's just it," said Jake. "No one wants to stand up for child rapists. But you have to wonder if castration falls under 'cruel and unusual punishment.'"

"Well, considering the crime…"

"Have you ever heard of convicted murderers being exonerated after decades in prison when DNA evidence proves them innocent?"

There was another moment of silence. "You can't give someone back twenty stolen years," I said.

"And you sure can't give them their balls back." Jake gave us a look, and I instinctively covered my crotch. "Who's most likely to be convicted?" he continued.

"Black folks?" Andy answered. "Poor folks?"

"And if this law goes into effect?"

I felt a chill. We all knew that the far right already considered every LGBTQ person a child predator. There could be horrific consequences with such a law even if the U.S. didn't face a complete takeover. Individual far-right states could still inflict enormous damage on their own.

A vague memory of something I'd read years ago started coming back to me. "Weren't a lot of black and indigenous women forcibly sterilized in the twentieth century?" I asked. I remembered hearing the number 70,000. Or was it 100,000? Maybe more?

"And I think something like a third of all women in Puerto Rico," Jake told us.

That *couldn't* be true.

Could it?

"We hardly need fascism to be awful to one another," Andy said.

"But full-fledged fascism will sure make it easier," Jake reminded us.

"It's late," I said, "and I'm beat after all the sex we've had lately. But if we might only have a few more months to use our testicles…"

"Use 'em before we lose 'em?" Andy asked with a raised eyebrow.

I stood and held out my hand. Andy and Jake stood, too, and we headed to the bedroom, forcing ourselves to have fun.

Twice.

Chapter Twelve: Santino

I'll spare you the graphic details this time. There was nothing repulsive involved, though I suppose repulsive is in the mouth of the beholder. [And there's no way to explain what I mean by that without going into graphic detail, so...]

Besides, it was what happened next I need to record. Just as I was licking the last of Andy's cum off Jake's back, I saw something out of the corner of my eye and looked off to the side of the bed. The side Andy wasn't on.

"Fuck!"

"What?" Jake turned over quickly and seemed to see what I was seeing. "Who are you?"

It was the man I'd seen briefly in the mirror the other day. Now that he remained visible for more than an instant, I could get a better look. Impressive enough that even the flash I'd seen before had created a pretty accurate memory.

The man was just over six feet tall, with clipped, medium brown hair—technically brunet, though we usually preferred it a tad darker—with a beard that alone made up for any other defects. About three quarters of an inch deep, it was fuller than Andy's. I could tell it was soft, even from this distance.

And then there were the muscles. Lots and lots of muscles, straining against his T-shirt, worn deliberately two sizes too small.

"My name's Owen," he said. "I've been trying for days to make people see me. You're the only folks I've had any luck with so far."

"I saw you at Roland's house," I said.

"I saw you in the staff bathroom at work," Jake said.

This guy sure hung out in a lot of bathrooms.

"So who are you anyway?" I asked. "Can anyone else see you? Why are you showing up here?"

Owen frowned.

"Not that we mind," I added quickly. "You're quite the sight to behold." Both Jake and Andy nodded in unison. "And we obviously have no bias against ghosts."

"Some of your best friends, huh?"

"We just don't understand how any of this works."

Owen shrugged. "I didn't get a manual either."

"It doesn't appear you wasted away from disease," Jake prompted.

You know how it is when a partner gives you a "look"? It's the same when a ghost does it.

"It was a Sunday," Owen finally began. "I'd just left my apartment to go for a bike ride."

I couldn't help but notice his eyes briefly surveying my paunch.

"I ride a couple of hours on weekends," he continued. "On other days, I usually just head to the gym. But weekends, I like to bike."

"So what happened?" asked Jake. "You didn't have a heart attack, did you? You look like maybe you use steroids?"

"Some," he admitted. "But I started out, how can I say, naturally gifted. Most of this—" He flexed. "—is the real me."

"Were you killed?" asked Andy. "Maybe it's people who're murdered who become the ghosts that hang around."

"I was hit by a car from behind," Owen said. "Not really murder. Manslaughter, I suppose. Just some idiot texting. You'd be surprised how often that happens, even with all the bike lanes in Seattle. I try to be careful." He shrugged. "But you can't live in fear."

Jake and I had both remained sexually active at the height of the AIDS epidemic, hadn't we? People did what they needed to do to feel alive.

"Did they catch him?"

"Or her." He shook his head. "I don't really know. Those first few days were way confusing. And I didn't know where to go." He glanced at Andy and then turned back to me. "I mostly hung out at the bathhouse on Capitol Hill. Plenty of room to nap. And lots of guys to watch when it gets busy."

"Can you participate?" asked Andy. "Or do you just watch?"

[And now we were back to talking about sex.]

"Oh, I can get inside a man when I want to," he replied. "I haven't tried directing the action. That feels, I don't know, invasive." He laughed. "But no hall monitor ghosts have come by and wagged their finger at me."

If there was one thing we knew as gay men—non-monogamous gay men—it was that moral guidelines weren't always hard and fast.

"I just let the man do whatever he wants," Owen went on, "and go along for the ride. So far, everything feels...heightened."

None of us quite knew what to say to that, but I remembered Andy's experience on light rail. "You can stay here," I finally managed. "No sex required." I turned to Andy and Jake. "We get more than enough."

"Though I doubt any of us would turn you down."

Owen laughed again. I could see smile lines now, too distracted by his other features to notice before. "I've been watching you three for the past few days. I'm not the marrying kind, but you guys look good together."

While that didn't sound like either a no or a yes, there was no need to clarify for now. "Thank God we have a king size bed," I said. "We bought it for the occasional orgy, but it works for...whatever this is, too."

The next morning, Andy and I saw Jake off to work. Owen headed out "to do his own thing," making the obvious pun. My husband, unfortunately, had to work five days a week. The dental clinic where I worked was open four days a week, and I only worked three. We needed my full-time income, but working part-time was our compromise. It was either part-time work or clinical depression, and this seemed the lesser of two evils. Less money to enjoy life, but more time to enjoy what little I could.

This morning, as usual, I spent a few minutes reviewing the headlines and the first three or four paragraphs of stories I felt it would be irresponsible not to know at least the minimum about. But my attention was also grabbed by an article on reducing stress. "Top 6 Things You're Doing to Avoid Stress That Actually Increase It."

Okay, worth a quick read.

You wanted to avoid making a wrong decision and feeling bad about it, but you shouldn't over research small matters. You wanted to make sure to get enough rest, but you shouldn't keep hitting the Snooze button. You wanted to displace negative thoughts, but you shouldn't binge shop to stay occupied because you'll end up with a bill.

Sheesh.

Someone actually got paid to write that, I thought. Perhaps I could earn a few bucks to put toward our "10 Things to Do Before the Apocalypse" list by submitting an article called "Top 6 Listicles That Are Totally Useless."

I joined Andy on the porch. Our home was view-adjacent. We could see the Ethiopian Christian church across from us but not much else. If we walked down the front steps, we could see the downtown Seattle skyline. If we walked to the middle of the street, we could see the Cascades.

But Jake and I had planted yellow daffodils and red tulips and purple iris and blue hydrangea in our front yard. Lavender and rosemary and grape hyacinth and California lilac. Even a messy camellia. Something was always blooming.

"Top 8 Flowering Plants That Hold Their Ground Against Weeds."

"You know," Andy said as we sat on the porch, watching Mason bees flit about, "we could head to my bank today and *you* could ask questions I can't."

"Why would they talk to me?"

"Because you'd be applying for an equity loan."

The pain that immediately pierced my chest gave me a fright, but I realized quickly enough I was only horrified by the idea of additional debt and was not actually having a heart attack. I was about to suggest we find some other ruse when it struck me this might be a way of temporarily easing our financial stress. We could go through a few more items on our list of things to do before the apocalypse. Maybe even have enough to buy plane tickets if the election didn't go well in November.

If fascists really did take over, they'd eventually find "legal" ways to confiscate our property.

"The mortgage department starts taking calls at 9:00," Andy said.

I looked at my watch. "That gives us another twenty minutes." I looked at Andy. "What do you suppose we could do in twenty minutes?"

[Santino's a bit wordy, if you haven't noticed. We decided at the start we'd split the story evenly, but he keeps hogging extra chapters.]

[Okay, I'll refrain from sharing the details of the next forty minutes, only saying we ended up showering together afterward. And point out that this edit proves beyond any shadow of a doubt gay men are capable of self-control.]

[Libidinous self-control or loquacious self-control?]

[Stop editing my edits!]

[My input should count as much as anyone else's. This is a democratic throuple, right?]

[Do you want to be right or do you want to be happy?]

[I'm shutting up.]

Banks being the predatory institutions they are, the loan officers found an open appointment for us at 1:00. Since we had a couple of free hours, Andy and I strolled through Kubota Garden before walking down the hill to Safeway to grab a few things for dinner.

The few times Jake and I had managed to enjoy a short vacation in Europe, we made sure to dedicate half our time doing "normal" activities to get a taste for what it might be like to live there. As much as we enjoyed museums and other touristy things, everyday things in Paris or Milan or Vienna were even better.

Heading across the parking lot, Andy pointed. "Bus is coming."

We started hurrying but then came upon an ancient man inching along in his walker. "Arnnhnnhm!" he yelled at us as we passed.

A stroke victim. Out on his own. He motioned weakly toward the bus stop and moaned again.

I'd have to take his moan for it. "Let's try to help him," I said. "Can you grab an arm?"

When Andy reached for him, the man looked him in the eyes. God only knew what that meant for this poor soul, but I grabbed the man's other arm, and together Andy and I lifted/dragged/helped the guy continue inching his way toward the bus stop. Six inches at a time now instead of one.

We all missed that bus, but the 7 was scheduled every ten minutes at this time of day, and inchers couldn't be choosers. Andy and I chatted with the man, a rather one-sided conversation, until the next bus pulled up and we helped him board.

Andy and I still arrived for our appointment in plenty of time. You can't rely on public transit and not factor in a buffer.

We sat at Marilyn's desk, and she brightly began explaining the benefits of the different types of equity loans. "You guys look busy," I said, motioning toward Andy's desk at his suggestion. "Someone out on vacation?"

Marilyn's smile tightened. "One of our staff moved on to greener pastures," she said, still with the fake smile.

I put my hand on my chest. "Oh, thank God!" I pretended to chuckle. "I heard someone here had been murdered."

Marilyn froze. I really wasn't very good at detecting. "That must have been someplace else," she managed to say before asking for additional information so she could pull my credit report. Andy wandered off to his manager's office but came out a few minutes later shrugging.

I couldn't just hope people would start randomly offering relevant information unprovoked, so I tried again. "I heard that the guy who was killed had turned down a coworker's advances."

Marilyn stopped typing mid-word and stared at me. *Cold.* I'd never felt so frightened in my life.

Until thirty seconds later.

"What the hell are *you* doing here!" Roland Kronenberg barged into the mortgage department.

"I'm getting a loan," I said, my voice hardly quivering at all. "What about you?"

"I'm here to pick up my *husband's* belongings. They're mine now." He stalked over to Andy's abandoned desk and opened a thick, black plastic garbage bag before swiping items off the top of the desk into it. He opened a drawer and grabbed more items.

"We'll have to go through that," said a woman I assumed was Bouchra, exiting a tiny office at the far end of the room. "Make sure there's nothing confidential."

"You've had plenty of time for that." Roland shoved a few more items into the bag. He looked like Bad Santa.

Marilyn tapped her desk loudly, and I turned to face her. "Can we get back to your loan?"

"Oh, um, sure."

Roland stormed past us, deliberately bumping my shoulder with the bag of Andy's personal items. Two feet past, he turned and spat in the general direction of the office. "I'll be selling our house and I'm *not* using you guys!"

He turned to leave, and just at that moment, music began blaring from someone's computer. John Legend singing the beautiful but haunting lyrics from "All of Me." Roland turned and stared, his face blanching. A man a couple of desks over hit several keys on his computer frantically, and the music died.

Roland almost tripped as he hurried away, just as a security guard arrived to see what the fuss was all about.

"I apologize for taking so much of your time, Marilyn," I sputtered, "but I'm going to think about this loan a little longer. Please don't run my credit yet." I picked up my bag of groceries.

Andy gave me an encouraging smile, and my heart slowly stopped racing. We headed to the door, out of the building, and toward the bus stop.

"Whew!" I placed my hand on my chest as if that would slow my heart rate. I could feel my Do Not Resuscitate pendant against my sternum.

"Shall we go home and debrief?" Andy asked with a laugh.

"Did we actually learn anything?" I asked. All I saw was that Andy might well miss life itself but he wasn't likely to miss many of the people who had filled up that life.

"We learned we need to ask better questions," he said. "And ask them faster." He paused. "Maybe I'll have you set up a new email account and send folks an anonymous email. The police could track the IP if it came down to that, but you won't be sending threats. Just insinuations to make people nervous."

I nodded. "We'll do that as soon as we get home," I said. "But first, let's try to find someone down on Pioneer Square to give this food to."

Chapter Thirteen: Jake

"Look at them," Kelton said, nodding toward the shoppers wheeling carts of two by fours and paint cans and faucets.

"Yeah?" My coworker Kelton was young, early thirties, worked out at the gym, and wore a cologne that telegraphed his intention to keep working his way up the ladder at the company.

"All those fat men," he scoffed, "thinking they're any good at DIY projects."

I'd long since stopped worrying about Kelton's opinion of my body and could usually ignore his comments about others, too, focusing instead on my work. Today, though, thinking about Andy's no-longer-in-existence body, I wanted to point out some flaw on Kelton's, or at least make him feel less secure about judging.

Perhaps I could ask Owen for a photo I could place on my desk. Everyone here knew I was gay. No reason I couldn't let them think whatever they wanted when I talked about my "good, really good friend, Owen."

A photo that let me see his studly ears whenever I wanted.

Unfortunately, while Kelton was not especially well built, he also had no visible flaws, and I had little desire to check out his Grindr profile. Besides, he'd hardly post anything negative there. Though I expected he was scowling in his profile pic. Most gay men were. Cheerfulness apparently wasn't sexy.

"If we only allow shoppers with 15% body fat," I said, "we'll go out of business pretty fast."

Kelton snorted. "Don't they even *care*?"

"About your disgust?" I asked. "Probably not." I almost turned back to my work but decided to add what I hoped was a final comment. "We could tell them how you feel if it's that important to you. Use the store's loudspeaker."

Kelton's eyes narrowed. "You are so mean sometimes."

I chuckled, though the amusement didn't last long. Right now, we were coworkers, but I was well aware that within a year he'd probably be senior to me.

Tina Fey had recently released a remake of *Mean Girls*. I couldn't help wonder who might star in the adaptation *Mean Gays*. Way too many gay men seemed forever stuck with a junior high attitude: snarky, critical of what others wore, of their hair style, dissing every "flaw" they perceived in another man's body, imitating Simon Cowell when reviewing their performance in bed.

Being bitchy might garner a laugh, but it wouldn't make anyone like you. Anyone willing to say nasty things about others who have never even bothered them will without a doubt say them sooner or later about you, too.

Plenty of great gay men out there, of course, but running into them often felt rather like encountering meteoroids in the

Earth's orbit. Lots of open space between them. The only good thing about these interactions with Kelton was that they reminded me how fortunate I was to be with Santino.

And Andy.

Finding *two* wonderful men felt more preposterous than running into a ghost. Every few days.

I called home on my next break. "Santino, you and Andy having a good day?"

"I filmed us having sex this afternoon," Santino said.

"How did it go?" I asked, wondering if Owen had joined in. But he was just an acquaintance at this point. At best, he might become a friend like Tyler or Osman or Craig. Perhaps platonic, perhaps sexual. But now that we did know another ghost, I kind of hoped he'd stay in our lives, in whatever capacity worked.

Psychotic break, anyone? I suppose I'd always wonder. The same way I did about my paunch. Most of the time, I had a reasonably good body image, but once in a while, the insecurities and doubts flooded in.

"*We* can see us," Andy explained. Santino had obviously put his phone on Speaker. "But I expect other folks would just see Santino masturbating in a very odd position."

I laughed. I'd known calling them would put me in a better mood.

Then they recounted the other things they'd done today. "Yikes," I said. Suddenly, spending so many hours with Kelton felt trivial. I hated to be spending more money again so soon, but we needed a treat tonight. "Want to eat out this evening?"

"The restaurant on Second?"

"Why not?" Sleuthing might reduce the treat aspect of the meal, but it had to be done at some point. "8 Things to Do to Pretend We're Making an Effort."

I went home after work, listening to the news along the way. Over two hundred people had drowned in flooding in Kenya, Republicans were fighting a Democratic effort to replace lead water pipes, the bronze plaque memorializing those killed in the Upstairs Lounge fire in New Orleans had been stolen, and over two thousand anti-genocide protesters had been arrested on college campuses across the U.S.

Oh, and Trump was now selling his "God Bless the USA" bible, which included the Bill of Rights, the Declaration of Independence, the Constitution, and Lee Greenwood's song lyrics.

"Let's not talk about the news," I suggested as the three of us headed to the bus stop. We kept telling ourselves this, but it wasn't as easy as snapping our fingers. Keeping my worries to myself and not communicating was a sure way to chip away at our marriage. I didn't want either Santino or Andy hiding their concerns, either.

But worries needed a window that could be opened or closed if we wanted to maintain the inside temperature on our sanity. So instead, we caught up more on each other's personal history. You didn't get to be our age without having a lot of stories to tell, but the older we got, the less other people wanted to hear them.

There was the time Santino and I came home from work and found thirty-five bees in our bathroom, with even more flying about outside the bathroom window. They'd found a hole in the siding and decided Santino and I had created a homey enough atmosphere that they wanted to move in with us. We waited another half hour until dusk, watching the bees settle down on the windowsill and go to sleep, and then gathered them into a cup and set them down outside. Santino then climbed a ladder and stuffed some insulation into the hole they'd been using to get in. The following day when more bees returned, they buzzed around for a short while, gave up, and moved on.

Santino and I could talk about that incident and others whenever something reminded us of the events. "Remember how the next morning I went into my office at the front of the house to check my email before work, and I heard humming?"

"Yeah. You thought bees were trapped between the blinds and your window, but it turned out to be the Ethiopian Christians across the street singing."

"It was 6:00 a.m.! It's ungodly to be up at that hour!"

But really, unless you were there, the story wasn't particularly interesting. It's one of the things that made a shared history with a partner so pleasant. You undoubtedly heard certain stories way too many times, but you also had a kind of secret language—words, gestures, phrases—that communicated an entire conversation no one else but you understood.

Like the cryptophasia of identical twins.

Santino and I held back on our history now and tried to catch up on Andy's. We didn't want his part of the partnership to feel inferior to ours because we had less shared time together with him. I was glad the two of them had spent some time alone today. It would help if right from the start, Santino and Andy had some shared history I wasn't part of. I'd need to spend some time with him alone, too. This way, we'd *all* be at a disadvantage when some stories came up. It wouldn't always be Andy who had to catch up. Santino and Andy would need to fill me in sometimes or Andy and I would need to fill Santino in.

"I was an extra in a movie once," Andy said. "I could hardly wait for the movie to be released."

"How did you look?" I asked.

"Out of focus." He grunted. "It was one of those scenes where the camera has the star's face in clear focus while the folks in the background are blurry."

"Well, that seems rude."

"I was trapped on an elevator one evening with a straight couple and their two dogs who needed a bathroom break."

"The couple or the dogs?"

"The dogs first," Andy said, "but the alarm button didn't work, the couple hadn't brought their cell phones, and mine didn't have enough juice."

"Uh oh."

"There was soon plenty of juice everywhere."

"Ewww!"

Andy told several more brief stories, and Santino and I threw in a couple of our own anecdotes. If one of us went on too long, though, the other would tap the back of our hand. Our signal to shut up.

"Then there was the first time I had sex with Roland," Andy said. "It was quite unnerving."

"Big dick?" I asked.

"Little dick?" Santino asked.

"Average dick?"

"Two dicks?"

"I see someone's been hoping for some genetic engineering," Andy said. "You're right that it was his dick that surprised me, but it was the color."

"Excuse me?"

"He had a couple of large red wine birthmarks along one side." He shrugged. "I'm afraid I don't have any pictures. He refused to take any or let me take one."

"It must not have been *too* unnerving," I pointed out, "since you stayed."

"Looked kind of like a Holstein cow, if the colors were different."

"Maybe a Guernsey?" I suggested. I remembered the classic *Star Trek* episode where two men fought because one half of their body was black and the other half white, only the colors were reversed. One man was white on his right side and the other was white on his left side. Unacceptable.

Andy absentmindedly scratched at his crotch. "I just wish he'd given me a heads up. It's hard to stay in the mood when you're trying to decide if that's someone's natural coloring or if he has an STI."

"How long did it take you to figure it out?" Santino absentmindedly scratched at his crotch, too.

"I came right out and asked. He said he was afraid to tell me ahead of time. Other guys had refused to go home with him."

"He could at least have told you once you were in the bedroom."

"Roland made me undress first. Told me later that even if I decided not to have sex, he'd at least have gotten to see me naked."

"How…thoughtful."

Andy shook his head. "I missed a lot of red flags."

"So to speak."

"I tried to talk him into getting a tattoo, but he didn't want one. And then I got to thinking I should get one." He looked out the window. "But…"

The loss of shared history was part of what made losing loved ones so awful. No more "Remember that time when…" Nope. No one remembered anymore but you. Most of us felt alone at times even in the best of relationships, but now that feeling became your new partner. *You* were still alive, but so much of your life was now trapped alone inside your head, making you feel you were walking around with an ankle monitor, free but not free.

I reached over and squeezed Andy's hand while reaching forward to squeeze Santino's shoulder.

A few minutes later, we reached our stop, climbing the steps from the Pioneer Square light rail station to street level and then heading down to Second Avenue. A weeknight, the restaurant was only half filled. When we were directed to a tiny table for two, Santino requested a table for four. "We might have a friend join us," he explained.

The server tried to keep a blank face but failed, the tiniest flash of exasperation flitting across his eyes.

"That's the same server from last time," Andy whispered.

I looked at the man's nametag. Faris. All I could think of was Anna Faris's character in *Mom*. Christy. Or, when she was tired of her pronunciation being corrected by the wife of the man she was sleeping with, "Christ-ee."

Our server Faris had small ears. Well-formed but too small for his head. Their presence begged other questions.

"What would you like to eat?" I asked Andy. "I'll order it and you can eat from my plate."

"Will I be able to?"

"You eat at the house, don't you?"

"But in public…"

"You can touch the table, can't you? You'll be able to eat the food." I turned to Santino and then back to Andy. "Whether everyone else in here sees the food stay on the plate or not, I don't know and I don't care."

I ordered the halibut while Santino ordered a cheeseburger with fries. I could hardly blame him for wanting a night off from healthy eating. We'd vowed years ago never to shame each other when it came to sex, food, political action, or anything else. We'd never even felt the need. The post-nup was just in case.

It was *really* hard not to ask for a bite of his burger.

We caught up some more on Andy's history while we waited for the food to arrive. Turned out we'd all had sex with a Catholic priest at some point, we'd all had sex with a Mormon missionary, and we'd all had sex with a Republican political canvasser.

To be fair, Santino and I had done both the priest and the Republican as threeways, so perhaps the coincidence wasn't all that surprising.

"The only one I caught crabs from," Andy informed us, "was the canvasser."

"I'd never do something like that now," Santino said. "Back then, I used to feel a bit of sympathy for oppressed men who'd felt forced to stay in the closet. But I won't sleep with the enemy anymore. If they want to defect and free themselves, we can negotiate."

Faris set our meals down on the table, gave us an odd look, and walked away.

"He looks Muslim," Andy said, "but who knows?"

"And if he is, he could still be gay and closeted."

"Or gay and out. Not all Muslims are conservative any more than all Jews are ultra-Orthodox."

"I don't even worry about it when I talk to someone Jewish," I said. "I know so many secular Jews and don't particularly mind offending Jews who think gays are evil."

"But when you talk to a Muslim?" Andy asked.

I waited for Andy to take a bite of the fish and then took a bite myself. "I don't know," I said. "I'm always wondering if they hate Americans. If they assume I'm Christian and they hate Christians. Then I wonder if they have no problem with non-Muslims but are worried that *I* have a problem with *them*. Does someone like Faris hate us? Does he think we hate him? So many Christians want us dead because we're gay, so am I overreacting to worry that Muslims want us dead, too?" I waited for Andy to take another bite of the fish. "I know it means I'm biased," I continued, "but every time I interact with a Muslim, or someone I think might be Muslim, there's this…ghost in the living room."

"Is it real?" Andy suggested. "Is it my imagination?"

I nodded and took a sip of my tea.

"Do you think he killed me?" Andy asked. "Maybe called a friend to wait for me outside because my existence struck him as especially objectionable?"

"It feels Islamophobic to even ask the question."

Santino shrugged. "Isn't that like Netanyahu framing every criticism of Israeli war crimes as antisemitic? I mean, there are Christian murderers and Jewish murderers and atheist murderers. Why wouldn't there be Muslim murderers, too?"

We debated the ethics of asking Faris to talk to us during his break or after work and decided we'd risk the offense. When he came to pick up our plates, I broached the subject. "A friend of ours ate here a week and a half ago," I said, "and he was murdered shortly after leaving. I wondered if maybe you noticed anything odd with his coworkers. Or if you noticed anybody else in the restaurant who looked at him strangely or followed him out."

Too many questions to throw out all at once. I needed to pay more attention when we watched our detective shows.

Faris looked at me and let his eyes slowly move over to Santino's before turning back to me. "I don't know anything."

"Could we maybe talk after—"

The server left with our plates. A few moments later, a different server came over with our check. Okay then.

"I couldn't tell if he saw me or not," Andy said. "I could see right into his eyes when he was looking at us, but his face was so blank, I couldn't tell if he could see into *my* eyes."

We left cash on the table, including a generous tip, and stood. As we were leaving, Andy broke away and ran up to the kitchen door just as Faris was coming out. "Boo!" he shouted.

Faris paused, but then, another server was heading his way with a tray.

"Let's go," I said, motioning with my head.

When we stepped out onto the sidewalk, we were greeted by Detectives Gamroth and Degroen, standing there as if waiting just for us.

Chapter Fourteen: Andy

"Mr. Castellano," Detective Gamroth said, nodding pleasantly. "Mr. Maddox."

"Um, hello detectives," Jake managed.

"What brings you here tonight?" she asked. "And please don't say you were hungry."

We all moved aside a bit to make sure the sidewalk was clear for other pedestrians. "I hope I didn't get you guys in trouble," I whispered.

"We know Andy ate his last meal here," Santino said, "and we wanted to see if anyone looked suspicious." Detective Gamroth and Detective Degroen looked at Jake and Santino without saying anything. "Simple as that," Santino added. The pause afterward seemed to linger. Detective Degroen looked away first, his eyes tracking a young woman walking past with her boyfriend.

"I see," Detective Gamroth said slowly. "And *did* you notice anything suspicious?"

"Not…really," Jake admitted.

"No one returning to the scene of the crime?" she pressed.

"Is that really a thing?" asked Santino.

She nodded. Jake and Santino seemed at a loss for words. I was, too, trying to suggest something for them to say. Detective Gamroth turned to her partner and then back to us. "Funny," she said, "but *I* happened to notice something suspicious."

"Yeah?" Santino swallowed. "I mean, yes?"

"Detective Degroen and I were heading back here to ask a couple of follow up questions, and when we looked in the window, we saw two people who have already acted oddly...acting quite oddly."

"Eating a cheeseburger isn't odd."

Considering how Jake and Santino usually preferred healthier meals, I thought it probably was.

Detective Gamroth looked at my friends a second too long. "But talking to an empty chair is."

"We, um, wanted to pretend Andy was still here," Jake said. "Have a last meal with him." He rubbed the back of his head.

"And you couldn't do that at home?" Detective Degroen finally asked his first question. He looked at his watch briefly before becoming distracted again by two women entering the restaurant.

Jake straightened, looking a bit taller. "Frankly, we do it at home, too. But we wanted to come here tonight where, um, he had his last meal?"

There was another long pause before Detective Gamroth spoke again. "Have you talked to a grief counselor?" she asked. "People grieve in different ways, but this…" She motioned toward the restaurant, "isn't what homicide detectives feel inclined to dismiss."

"Dr. Thornton!" I hissed. "Tell them you're going to see Dr. Thornton!"

"Uh…"

"He's my psychiatrist," I hurried. "For occasional depression. Tell them you've looked up a good psychiatrist and plan to call soon."

"You okay, Mr. Maddox?"

Jake repeated what I'd suggested as calmly as possible. I saw Detective Degroen write something down. He was missing part of a finger. Had I noticed that before?

He glanced at his watch again.

"I'd make an appointment sooner rather than later," Detective Gamroth said. She paused another moment and then nodded before she and her partner continued into the restaurant.

"Jesus Christ!" Jake whispered.

"Holy shit!" whispered Santino.

"Should you guys be cursing at an empty spot on the sidewalk?" I asked.

We started back toward the light rail station. A homeless man watching us talk to an "imaginary" friend paused as he approached and then crossed the street.

"Maybe this would be a good time to put our Operation Evacuate into effect," Santino suggested. "Leave the country."

"We don't have enough money saved," Jake said. "We're not ready."

While fiddling on Bouchra's computer the day before, I'd read an article in the *New York Times* about politicians in DC discussing at parties what countries they planned to flee to if Trump won again in November. Gallows humor was one thing, but this wasn't normal.

"It would be like announcing your guilt," I said.

I'd read some Isaac Bashevis Singer in college, stories of a vibrant, complicated culture. That world of Eastern European Jewry was completely wiped out in just a few years. Some Jews survived, and Judaism itself survived, but that world was gone forever.

"We're crap at this detecting stuff," Santino said, "but we'll have to keep trying. We need to find out who killed you, for all our sakes."

Back at the house an hour and fifteen minutes later, we settled down on the sofa, my head on Jake's lap, with Santino rubbing my feet, and watched an episode of *Dead Like Me*.

***

"Woo-ooo-ooo!"

I blinked my eyes open. The lights were out. It was the middle of the night. I could feel Jake and Santino's bodies pressed against me.

"Woo-ooo-ooo!"

Jake reached over and turned on the bedside lamp. Owen stood beside the bed, waving his hands dramatically. "Scared?" he said, grinning.

"Fucker," Santino mumbled.

Owen shrugged. "That's what I'm hoping. I get tired of just watching over at the bathhouse. Even when I join in, I can never join in as *me*."

The three of us scooted up to lean against the headboard. "You'd want to have sex with us?" Jake asked. "I mean, with me? I don't want to project my doubts onto these guys, but I don't seem your type."

"And what's my type?" Owen raised an eyebrow.

"Not sure which religious tradition," Jake said, "but definitely a god of some sort."

"Well, I'm not a narcissist, you know."

"Hey," Santino said, "low blow."

Owen caressed his beard and patted his hard stomach as he surveyed us, chuckling. "If I could only have sex with men who look like me, I wouldn't have many to choose from, would I."

It wasn't a question. "Someone has a healthy self-image," I said.

"Do you disagree?"

How could I? How could any of us?

Owen shrugged. "It's okay to be honest." He motioned to himself. "I've got a great body. But if I wanted to have sex with myself, I'd use my hand, a dildo, or one of those flashlight thingies."

"I've got one if…" Santino pointed to his bedside table with a thumb.

"I'm attracted to a wide variety of men," Owen continued. "That's why I'm single."

"You can be promiscuous even in a committed relationship," Jake pointed out.

"No argument there," Owen said. "It's just that some folks are meant to be coupled, some to be part of threesomes, some in other kinds of polyamorous relationships." Owen started taking off his underwear. "And some of us do best by staying single."

I'd say my first human/ghost orgy was everything I'd dreamed of. Only I'd never dreamed of such a thing in my life.

Only in my death.

Chapter Fifteen: Andy

Wednesday morning, Owen told us he'd be catching a bus to Snoqualmie Falls to spend a day out in nature. He might be back later and might not. "Tomorrow, I might try to look again for whoever ran me over."

"You don't need to check in," Jake said. "We're hopefully becoming friends, but we understand the different expectations."

Santino headed back to the dental clinic and Jake called in sick to work. We stood on the porch and watched Santino walk over to Renton Avenue to catch the bus. Then we sat in their two metal rockers from the 1940s, painted a deep purple.

"We're going to have a good day," Jake told me. "We're going to do some one-on-one bonding, and the news is completely off limits until Santino gets home." He paused. "Maybe even then."

We'd already made the mistake of listening to the news before breakfast. A U.S. airman had self-immolated in front of the Israeli embassy in DC. Far-right legislators were attempting to ban contraceptives. They were trying to pass legislation to monitor women's menstrual cycles. Some wanted to ban no-fault divorce. A self-proclaimed white nationalist in Congress spoke of the need to execute "traitors." A second Boeing whistleblower had died under mysterious circumstances. The psychological blows kept piling up. And we'd only had the news on for ten minutes.

Maybe we *should* call Dr. Thornton.

"What's something you wish you had done but never got around to?" Jake asked.

I shrugged. "It's something I never even told Roland," I said. "But somehow, with you guys, I feel like my dick's already in your mouth. A little late to worry about head cheese."

"What you're saying," Jake enunciated carefully, "is that you wanted to write greeting cards?"

"Maybe once you're dead, you stop giving a fuck about certain things."

"Like embarrassment?"

"I wish...I'd tried karaoke at least once." I waited for the judgment, but it didn't come.

"Can you sing?"

"I don't know." I laughed. "I've never let anyone hear me besides me."

Jake held out his hand as if offering a candy. "No time like the present." He glanced around, and I saw a pretty Black woman in her forties, getting something out of her car next door. "It's not as if you're going to disturb the neighbors."

I blinked. "Sing *a capella*?"

"The birds won't mind, either." Jake gave an encouraging smile. "And if you're awful, I won't say a word to Santino. It'll be our secret."

I sighed, closed my eyes, looked at the last of the tulips in the front yard, sighed again, took a deep breath, and stood. There was one pop song I'd long enjoyed, listening to it often on YouTube, especially on evenings when Roland and I weren't speaking. Then I began the first lyrics from "I'm Yours," painfully aware I sounded nothing like Jason Mraz, and painfully aware that even Jason Mraz sounded better when accompanied by music.

Jake leaned forward and looked into my eyes as I sang, and somehow, I managed not to look away. I also managed to get through the entire song.

When I finished, I desperately needed some affirmation, even though I'd just said there was no point worrying about head cheese any longer.

Jake said nothing for a moment. I took a breath, and then he opened his mouth to speak.

"You listening to the radio?" the woman next door called out, and we turned over to look. She was peering in our direction with her hand shading her eyes, even though it was cloudy out. "Are you *singing*?" she continued.

"Um…"

"You know I direct a youth choir, right?"

Jake stood and descended the porch steps, walking over toward his neighbor. I followed. She didn't seem to see me, though she'd clearly heard me. "It's one of Santino's favorite songs," Jake told her. I noticed he didn't clarify the source of the singing.

"Well, you're very good," the woman said.

I wanted to ask her name, but Jake could hardly introduce us.

"Thanks, Kayleah."

I squeezed Jake's hand.

"It does my heart good to hear people sing," Kayleah went on. "Brings joy into the world."

"You'll let us know when you guys have your next concert?"

"You bet."

"You have a blessed day," Jake said. Kayleah said the same back, they waved to each other, and then we went into the house. "I forget sometimes," Jake told me once the door was closed, "that there are good people who are Christians, too." He chuckled, but it was a sad sound. "I mean, it's obvious, right? But I forget."

"She couldn't see me."

Jake ignored the comment, as that was obvious, too. "She used to volunteer as a preacher's secretary until the preacher gave a homophobic sermon. She talked to him about it afterward. Then she found another church. Not easy because her husband's got multiple sclerosis. He's in a wheelchair and had to adjust his support network. But he was on board with the switch."

"She told you this?"

"We were talking about allies needing to stand behind their allyship."

I turned to look toward the front door. "Feels odd to hope, doesn't it? I don't realize I've been living without much until it comes along unexpectedly."

"Santino and I are lucky," Jake said, "but even so, it's hard when you feel alone against the world."

"I wish I'd met you guys while I was still alive."

"Well, we're together now," Jake reminded me. "Let's go shower, get dirty, and shower again."

Like always, I'll try to spare you the graphic details. Suffice it to say that Jake did most of the talking while lying on his back in the sling. I rimmed him for over half an hour while he recounted various sexual escapades. You can tell a lot of stories in thirty minutes. Some were only slightly above run-of-the-mill, several others were too outrageous for me to include even if we were including all the sex talk, but there were a couple I simply can't resist including. Otherwise, it sounds like all we did that morning was chat, and while the talk on the porch and throughout the day was important to us, there *is* a different level of intimacy when sex is involved.

"So there were the five of us in the room," Jake said while I licked away. "And you know how it is," he continued. "Everyone likes a mouthful of cum, but it's hard to take sometimes if you've already cum yourself. So we staggered everyone's orgasm."

I murmured and continued tickling his asshole, my beard rubbing against his balls.

"We'd set up a tray of hors d'oeuvres beforehand," Jake said. "Crackers with cheddar cheese, tiny pieces of toast with jam."

"Mm-hmm."

"So the first guy would jack off onto as many of the hors d'oeuvres as possible, and the guys who hadn't cum yet would each try to eat one. Then the next guy would beat off onto more of the hors d'oeuvres, and the remaining guys would eat some more. And so on. Then by the time the last guy added his cum, the first guy had had long enough to become aroused again and got to participate in the snacking as well."

I lifted my head for a moment, well aware that even my relatively routine rimming this morning would be grounds for extreme moral panic in many quarters, much less what Jake was describing. It didn't even matter if I'd have wanted to participate in that particular activity or not. The point was that *they* did, and it was nobody else's business.

I wasn't into bondage, but some folks were, both gay and straight. Some people enjoyed S&M, which seemed impossible to enjoy. Fisting sounded downright horrific, from either partner's perspective.

To be perfectly honest, having sex with a woman also sounded quite unappealing, though I'd heard that lots of men—and women—loved it more than pretty much anything else.

I remembered taking a Human Sexuality course in college on a lark. It was one of those auditorium classes with hundreds of students. The day before the lecture on pornography, the instructor informed us that if we felt offended by sexual images, we were free to skip that class without penalty. Of course, the next day, every student was in attendance, plus several others who weren't even enrolled.

The instructor proceeded to show image after image on a screen. After each image, he'd pause and ask the same questions. "Who thinks this is erotic?" There'd be a show of hands.

"Who thinks this is pornographic rather than erotic?" There'd be another show of hands.

"Who thinks this type of image should be allowed?" More hands.

"Who thinks this type of image should be banned?" Still another group of hands.

The instructor showed images of naked women by themselves. A naked man by himself. Men and women in leather. In maid outfits. Heterosexual couples aroused. Heterosexual couples having vaginal intercourse. Heterosexual couples having anal intercourse. Heterosexual couples having oral sex, women going down on men and men going down on women. There was enough variety to keep the hour-long class going with image after image.

Huge, outraged gasps, even in this day and age, when two men, both flaccid, appeared on screen together.

The instructor concluded with one last question. "Who here wants someone else to decide for them what they can and can't see?"

Not a single hand went up.

The religious right not only wanted to control what we could read or see but also what we could do in bed. The only legal sex was to be sex Christian evangelicals thought proper. All else would be made a felony. If they could monitor women's menstrual cycles, they could monitor orgasms, too. As it was, the far right Speaker of the House boasted that he and his son received alerts about each other's internet usage to make sure neither of them looked at porn.

"Was that too much?" Jake asked, rubbing the back of his head. "Did I freak you out with the snack sex talk? It's not everyone's cup of tea."

So to speak.

"The fact that you're willing to bare your soul to me completely is the most erotic thing anyone's ever done." And then I headed back in while Jake continued telling his stories.

[You sure you don't want to write an article about the "Top 5 Ways to Upset Straight People"?]

[Some of this upsets gay people, too.]

[You're just hoping someone emails the university press and asks for contact information.]

[What good would that do me?]

[Well, for someone complaining about *me* being overly wordy, you've *also* started taking up a lot of space.]

[To keep your marriage brimming…]

After we showered and dressed, Jake and I headed for the bus stop. We spent a couple of hours at the Museum of Flight, with Jake splurging for two rounds in the flight simulator.

Since we were so close to where the 60 passed, we walked several more blocks to board and then headed to White Center to visit the adult video store. I honestly *will* spare you the details here, simply pointing out there's no real way to ask for consent when merging with someone in the gay theater. If the guy could see or hear me, he'd be able to feel me and we couldn't merge.

So I entered a guy who seemed anxious to interact with other viewers, and wow, was Owen right. We couldn't think each other's thoughts, but I did feel I had twice as many nerve endings as before. Every touch, every kiss, was electric. The taste of another man's skin [see? I didn't say cock] was raised to another level. All in all, it was quite the experience for me, and the middle-aged black man I'd merged with seemed to enjoy himself, too.

I wasn't going to inhabit someone every time I had sex, of course. Jake, Santino, and I all enjoyed our individuality. Possession sex—I was going to keep calling it "merging," which carried healthier connotations—would remain an option. Like giving blow jobs was an option, like fucking doggy style was an option, and so on. One more part of my sexual repertoire.

10 Things to Do Before the Apocalypse

Who knew I'd become so much more interesting sexually after I died?

On the way home, Jake and I stopped at the store and bought some crackers.

Chapter Sixteen: Santino

Jake and Andy had dinner ready when I walked through the door. Eggplant parmesan with veggie cheese. Palatable, not delicious. The good thing about palatable is that it was easy to decline seconds. A built-in weight loss regimen.

"Anything to talk about from work?" Jake asked.

"Nope."

Jake and Andy caught me up on their adventures of the day. Friends rarely believed us when we claimed we weren't jealous. My first reaction when Andy described the sex, and when Jake described the flight simulator, was to smile. "I'm so glad you guys had a good day!"

My second reaction was to feel grateful to be part of such a relationship.

We also checked the new email account. No one at all had replied to our anonymous insinuations. I hadn't really expected them to. I could only hope they'd read the emails and not deleted them outright. Pressure was still pressure.

Since Jake and Andy had cooked, I washed the dishes. Then we cuddled on the sofa while watching an episode of a French show, *The Returned*. The last thing either Jake or I wanted was to spend the entire evening every night watching television, so even for long shows or movies, we usually watched no more than an hour.

Tonight, as the show's closing credits scrolled on screen, I turned to the others. "What's next on the agenda?" Since they'd already had sex, I wasn't sure they'd be up for any more, and that was okay. It had been years since Jake and I had engaged in sex as often as we had these past few days.

"Let's price karaoke machines," Jake suggested.

"Really?" Andy sat up straighter.

"We've got music, we've got television, we have an exercise bike, we have a sling, and we have books. No reason not to add one more entertainment option," Jake replied.

"But…don't you need to save money for…?"

I joined the conversation again. "We've already looked into immigrating to Europe. I have an advantage with my Italian ancestry, but citizenship is only one part of the deal. We'd still need an income. There's a reason most visas require a guaranteed income of more than both our Social Security checks combined. And if there really is a fascist takeover, I can't imagine new laws wouldn't be passed banning gay people and lots of others from 'taking government money.'"

"We might end up refugees," Jake said, "but it's unlikely we'll ever be immigrants."

And given the rise of the far right in Italy, France, Sweden, and Germany, as well as in formerly unthinkable countries like Switzerland and Portugal, even if we were able to immigrate, it might not help.

"Unless a karaoke machine is outrageously expensive," Jake continued, "it might be a better investment to enjoy life now."

So we looked online and found that prices ranged from roughly $200 to $500. We could probably afford something on the lower end. "And are there any karaoke bars here?" Andy asked softly.

"Are you kidding?" I laughed. "Didn't Jake tell you about his humiliating experience on Capitol Hill?"

"I was trying to build confidence," Jake said, "not scare the man."

"Will you sing again if I do?" Andy asked.

He nodded. Andy smiled. And then I suggested our final activity for the evening. We straddled a padded bench—usually used for activities we won't go into here—sitting in a row behind one another. I rubbed Andy's back while he rubbed Jake's. We turned on a music playlist and rubbed each other's backs while listening to our favorite artists. After every three songs, the person in front would move to the back of the line while the other two moved forward.

We mostly rubbed in silence, though sometimes one or more of us would sing along. Other times, we'd chat about nothing in particular, no agenda other than enjoying one another's company. Since both Jake and I needed to work in the morning, bedtime approached sooner than we would've liked. Then Andy raised the subject of tattoos again.

"If you've made it this far without any ink," he said, "I'm guessing you're not planning to get tattoos."

I was in the most forward position on the bench at this point and shrugged. "A friend of ours got his first tattoo at seventy. Why?"

"I'll never be able to get the dragon tattoo I want," Andy said hesitantly, "but I could enjoy looking at a dragon on *your* cock."

My dick twitched nervously at the idea. It wasn't only the thought of several hours of pain while getting the tattoo that made me shiver but also the days of tenderness that would follow before the skin healed. But I already had more than enough regrets about things I'd failed to do in life. Perhaps it was finally time to try something "wild."

"If I get a tattoo," I said, "will you get one, too, Jake?"

"If you're getting a dragon, what should I get?"

"A motto on your butt."

"Pray tell."

"'Insert Firmly in Bottom.'"

"No, no. How about 'I Douched for You'?"

"Or 'Did You Know You Can Piss in Here, Too?'"

"Everybody wants to write greeting cards these days. Maybe we *can* work remotely from Europe, after all."

We took turns in the bathroom, brushing our teeth, pissing one last time—not in each other—before stripping and climbing into bed. A thought flashed through my mind I didn't like. Was I *glad* Andy had been murdered? He wouldn't be part of our throuple otherwise.

Then I thought about the Holocaust, because even alone in our minds, we all practiced Godwin's Law. People like Otto Frank remarried after the war, had other children. Holocaust survivors who relocated to Canada or the U.S. or Argentina met and married other survivors, people they loved and were happy to be with, people they'd never have met if so many others hadn't been murdered.

You couldn't really be happy about that, right? Yet it wasn't the same as making lemonade when life handed you a lemon. It wasn't "making the best of a bad situation."

Would there be happy gay couples, happy throuples, happy families, happy individuals five or ten years from now who would be happy because of the circumstances created if there was a fascist takeover in November?

Would there be a happy future for those who survived the death of the American empire? Who survived the death of capitalism? The death of the fossil fuel industry?

"5 Questions Not to Ask Yourself if You Want a Good Night's Sleep."

I pressed my ass into Andy's crotch and pulled Jake's ass into mine. We were spooning tonight, we were happy tonight, and that was all that mattered for now.

***

A steady beeping beat against my eardrums. It took a moment for me to realize it was the alarm clock. When I opened my eyes, the room was still dark, confusing. First light was visible even through our blinds by 6:00 a.m. these days.

"Which one of you fuckers set the alarm for the middle of the night?" I mumbled. Getting fucked at 3:00 a.m. was one thing, but no one had to wake me up for that. Jake had my permission to do whatever he wanted if he woke up randy during the night. I'd wake up as well the moment I was penetrated, of course, but if I felt Jake's arms around me, his weight on top of me, I could fall back asleep even as he pumped away.

If this was Andy's doing, we'd have to clarify the rules.

Jake and Andy were stirring now, too, groaning along with me. Then Andy shouted something unintelligible and leaped out of bed.

"Fire!" I finally heard him say. "The house is on fire!"

Jake and I scrambled to our feet, too, probably not wise, since that was where the most toxic fumes would be. But who could think that fast? I was still half asleep.

I didn't smell much. Maybe it was a false alarm. A bad battery. While Jake fumbled with his pants, I reached for the door handle. Cool to the touch. I carefully opened it, and then I could see the glow.

"Call 9-1-1!" I shouted.

I didn't bother to dress, simply scooped up my clothes, my phone, and my wallet. Then I headed for the hiding place where I kept my emergency documents—passport, birth certificate, and $1000 in cash, things I'd need in case of an earthquake, a fascist takeover, or a fire. Making sure Andy and Jake were behind me, I ran for the back door. The fire was somewhere at the front of the house.

We could already hear sirens by the time we made it along the side of our home and to the street. The nearest fire station was at the bottom of the hill, just past Kubota Garden. Thank heaven for small miracles.

"Did we turn the outside water on yet?" Jake shouted. We shut it off every winter so the pipes wouldn't freeze, and though it was now late spring, the weather hadn't yet turned warm and dry, so we hadn't needed to start watering the yard.

I dropped my things at Andy's feet and ran to the side of the house, twisting the valve for the garden hose. I pressed the nozzle and water burst out. Another bit of fortune. We weren't always so proactive. I quickly turned the stream on the porch, which was fully engulfed. Flames were almost certainly taking over the living room by now.

Goddammit.

Kayleah and her husband had come outside at the commotion. Eric rolled down their ramp, grabbed their garden hose, and aimed it at our porch as well. The sirens grew louder and louder, and I could hear both Jake and Andy shouting, but my mind was so full of chaos I couldn't make out a single word.

An eternity later, a fire engine pulled up in front of our house. Several men jumped out, and at that point, everything became even more of a blur. Someone pulled me back, perhaps Andy or Jake, and handed me my clothes. I dressed quickly. Then we huddled together, watching the firefighters save our home.

The flames were fully extinguished within ten minutes. Awful, but not nearly as awful as it might have been. We waited in a daze for what seemed like ages as the firefighters rummaged through the remains of the porch. Surreal. While there was some fire damage to the living room and edge of the roof, most of the damage inside was from smoke and water. Fortunately, it appeared most of that damage was limited to the front of the house.

A week ago, life had been normal.

We had insurance, though, and we weren't injured. But the next few months were still going to be unpleasant.

"You guys can stay in our spare room if you want," Kayleah offered. She and Eric had stayed outside with us for the past two hours, even though I knew she hated the cold, and it was chilly this morning, low fifties.

The house was livable, it seemed, but it would probably be off limits for a couple of days until the fire inspectors had finished investigating. Since there was no natural source of ignition on the porch, it was difficult not to believe the fire had been intentionally set. It was also difficult not to believe this was related to Andy's murder.

But it wasn't a given. Arsonists had set fires at the homes of several Asian American families in Kent and Federal Way over the past couple of months. A man had been caught on security video spraying a Black woman's car and front door with accelerant just last week up in Shoreline, setting them both on fire in the middle of the night. There was no reason haters couldn't have expanded their attacks to start including gay folks.

"Thanks, Kayleah," I said. "We may take you up on that. We'll let you know later today."

The sun was just starting to come up. Other neighbors strolled or drove by slowly to gawk. And then Detectives Gamroth and Degroen walked up the path. "Oh, um, hello," I said.

"Got a call this morning." Detective Gamroth nodded a greeting. "I've got your names on a list. I get pinged if they come up for anything—traffic stops or littering or…house fires."

I noticed Detective Degroen give Kayleah a lingering glance, flicking his eyes toward Eric half a second before returning his gaze toward Kayleah. And then back to us.

"Roland did this," Andy whispered. "I know it."

"If this turns out to be arson," Detective Gamroth continued, "do you think we'll find evidence that either of you bought an accelerant lately?"

"Excuse me?"

"Have you made an appointment with a psychiatrist yet?"

I closed my eyes.

"Uh huh." She surveyed the smoking, blackened porch. "Trying to deflect suspicion by making yourselves look like victims?" She glanced again at the front of the house. "Without actually doing too much serious damage?" Her eyes roamed a bit longer. "Maybe get an insurance settlement to make some improvements you wanted anyway?"

"You might want to question Roland," Jake suggested coldly. "He made a big fuss at the bank the other day. He could have looked up our address easily enough."

"You think Mr. Frey's husband set this fire?"

Jake shrugged. "It won't hurt to ask him."

"We're not going to do that," Detective Degroen said with a tone of finality. I couldn't tell if the expression on his face was weariness or disgust.

"And just why the hell not?"

"Because," Detective Gamroth took over again, "Roland Kronenberg is dead."

Chapter Seventeen: Jake

It wasn't easy turning down Kayleah's kind offer. Letting people help who wanted to help usually benefited both parties. Created a stronger bond. But it would've been impossible to avoid talking to Andy without being overheard. As a Christian, Kayleah would technically believe in "spirits," but when faced with the reality of gay men talking to invisible people in her home, it might be difficult to resist making…unflattering assumptions.

Andy offered to stay in our house if we chose to stay in the neighbors' guest room. It wouldn't be dangerous for him and he couldn't really contaminate any evidence. But we didn't want to be apart, not even that small distance. We also weren't up to "coming out" to any of our gay friends just yet.

By the time we finished up at the scene, light rail was running again after its usual late night closure. We headed out to Seatac and rented a hotel room near the airport. Lots of cheap hotels within walking distance. We took separate showers, way too tired to even think about sex, and plopped onto the bed.

It was after 11:00 before I opened my eyes again.

"He looks so innocent when he's sleeping," Andy commented, standing over me beside Santino, who was also peering down.

"Just like a little grandpa."

I stuck out my tongue.

"Put that away," Santino said. "No time for tongues right now."

I grumbled and sat up. Santino and Andy were both already dressed. Same clothes we'd stumbled out of the house with, of course. Before heading for the hotel, we'd also been allowed back in to grab our phones and a few other items. But no food. My stomach grumbled as loudly as I had a moment earlier.

I wanted coffee.

"If Roland's been murdered, too," Andy said, "then I couldn't have been killed by a random homeless person or drug addict or anything like that. It *has* to be someone at the bank."

"Could it have been your crow-hating neighbor?"

"Why would *they* be targeting you?" He shook his head. "It's someone *you've* met, too."

"Have you been able to talk to Roland?" I asked. "Has he come around?"

Andy shook his head again. "We don't have ghost GPS. Assuming Roland wanted to talk, he doesn't know where we are."

"Neither does Owen," Santino reminded me.

Even if Owen was to become a good friend, he wouldn't be checking in with us every day. He might do so more right now simply because he had no other options for conversation. Then again, he might be content going to the movie theater and watching one new release after another. Spending the day at the gym working out. He might be able to audit a college class.

"Maybe the investigators will let us back in later today." I crossed my fingers.

"What we need to do now," Andy said, "is head to the bank and make a scene. Spook the killer into taking action again."

"Can we get coffee first?"

"Only in a unionized store."

***

"I feel like we should synchronize our watches," I said, standing half a block down from Andy's bank.

"It's not *Mission: Impossible*," Santino chided.

"*Mission: Unlikely*?" I asked.

"I'll go in first," Andy interrupted. "I'll get on every computer in the mortgage department. Pull up a tab. Queue up 'All of Me' on each one. And as soon as you guys come in, I'll start hitting Play on one tab after another."

He gave us each a peck and headed inside.

It was difficult to feel scared after everything we'd been through lately. The killer wasn't going to attack us in front of all his or her coworkers. Besides, anger had a way of replacing fear. That wasn't necessarily healthy. Just a fact.

I wanted this bastard.

We waited ten minutes to give Andy time to pull up at least a few tabs. If his coworkers were on their computers every second, his access would be limited. But if his workplace was anything like mine, his coworkers were probably avoiding work as often as performing it.

We walked into the lobby and headed to the mortgage department, Santino leading the way. No one stood out as murderish. One man's ears stood out, though, as lickable. Andy saw me looking. "Brett," he said.

"You could have gone out with him at least once," I muttered under my breath.

"Can I help you?" asked a middle-aged woman. "Do you have an appointment?" Then she frowned. "Oh, you again?"

John Legend began singing "All of Me" on Marilyn's computer. She turned back toward her desk in confusion.

"We're here about the murder of Andrew Frey," Santino said loudly. The others in the office looked our way.

John Legend began singing "All of Me" on Brett's computer.

"And the murder of Roland Kronenberg," I added.

John Legend began belting out the lyrics to "All of Me" on Wickens's computer.

"We know who tried to murder us last night by burning down our home while we slept." Santino struggled to be heard over the music blaring throughout the office, the lyrics staggered as in a round. But he could always project better than I could.

John Legend now started singing from Bouchra's computer as well.

"Did you hack into our computers!?" Bouchra demanded. "Security!"

We turned around and walked out of the building before the guard could hear well enough to understand what the manager was asking. We hurried down the street and then quickly descended to the light rail platform at the Pioneer Square station and waited for the train.

I was shaking.

"What do you think?" Santino asked. "Did it work?"

"I'm about to pass out." Andy laughed. "And I'm not even guilty." He clapped me on the shoulder. "If the murderer was there, he's feeling the pressure."

"Anyone missing?" I asked.

"Petar. He's part-time."

"Well, he'll hear about what happened from the others, so if he's the guy, it'll just take a day or two longer to rattle him."

I hugged Andy, kissed him, and hugged him again.

"What's that for?"

"I'm scared if we find the killer, the universe will take you away."

Andy nodded, shrugged, and then hugged both of us. "I suppose this is what a soldier or police officer feels like putting their life on the line," he said. "Sometimes, you need to make a sacrifice for the greater good, as much as it sucks. 'Bravery' isn't even part of the conversation. Just doing what has to be done."

Like the protesters facing arrest and beatings and tear gas to fight the fossil fuel industry or genocide or abortion bans or any of the other issues we faced today.

But bravery definitely was required.

Andy might cease to exist altogether. He might end up in Hell. He might end up a caterpillar.

"If today could be our last day with you," Santino said, "we'd better not waste a second of it."

The train pulled into the station a few moments later, we boarded, and Andy sat down on top of an attractive young Indian listening to music. Santino and I sat a few seats away to watch as the two men merged, the young Indian man confused but not worried. Soon, he was smiling, a sense of fascination on his face as he bobbed his head to the music coming from his earpods.

Andy wanted to feel every sensation he could while he still had time.

We stopped for lunch at a vegetarian restaurant in Columbia City on our way home, spending way too much money yet again. The place served excellent food, though, a treat usually reserved for our birthdays or anniversary. We always laughed when we heard people asking if they could retire on a million dollars. Or four million. Or whatever other number they quoted that was astronomically out of our reach.

Could we retire on $11,000?

And, yes, we understood that even this represented privilege, that something like sixty percent of all U.S. households lived paycheck to paycheck and couldn't handle a single $500 emergency bill.

The American Dream used to be to purchase a home, to move up in the world, to have your children do even better. The dream now was not to end up in the gutter, bankrupt from medical debt or out of work due to downsizing or outsourcing.

Here we were in Seattle, one of the richest cities in the country, in one of the richest countries in the world, one of the richest cities in the history of civilization, and we couldn't find a way to fund public transit. Our public libraries were closing one day a week because they couldn't afford to stay open every day.

We had the money. More than enough. We just let rich people hoard it.

Because not only were corporations considered "people," so was capitalism itself. It was King Midas, wanting gold so badly it was starving itself to death.

"Um, I thought this meal was supposed to be a treat," Andy said after I spewed out my last bit of commentary. He handed my kimchi black bean burger back to me, probably hoping to shut me up.

I nodded. "I'm sorry. I…"

Santino continued eating his tofu/quinoa/pinto beans/pickled red onion mix. He'd heard my rants before.

"I see Dr. Thornton for a reason," Andy said. "It's hard to keep thoughts from spiraling sometimes. People watch the news for the bad stuff, not the good stuff. We rubberneck for traffic accidents, not a field of heather." He put his hand on mine. "Drugs aren't the only addiction."

"But it's like being addicted to food, isn't it?" I asked, looking at my burger. "You can't just never eat again. So how do you make sure you eat in moderation?"

"You spice your food with humor," Andy said.

"I…"

"It's like those cookies you make. A balance of ingredients to make them good but not great."

"But how does that work in reality and not just as a metaphor?"

"When I was at my mom's wake," Andy said, "I ran into some of her friends. They told some funny story, not about my mom. I can't even remember what the story was. But I laughed. And when they saw me laughing, they all got a horrified look on their faces. They stopped talking, stood around nervously a few more moments, and then walked off."

"Ouch."

"I wanted to tell them, 'I can cry anytime. What I need tonight is to laugh.' But some people don't want you to laugh."

"And instead of laughing, we've been using sex to relieve the pressure."

"Nothing wrong with that," Andy said. "In fact, I highly recommend it for recently murdered people."

"To be fair," Santino interrupted, "sometimes the way we have sex does make us laugh." He arched one of his brows.

"Only when your foot gets caught in the stirrup," I said, almost smiling. One didn't need to be bipolar or on street drugs to have mood swings these days.

"Or when one of your pubic hairs gets caught between my teeth," Santino added, the corner of his lips turning up as well.

"There was that time you pulled your back while fucking me and I had to crawl with you stuck inside me like a dog until I could reach the phone and call for help."

"But," Santino assured Andy, "we always keep our phones within easy reach now."

"You know, Jake," Andy said, "it's okay to have sex, even if other people in the world are suffering. It's okay to watch a movie. It's okay to listen to music. It's okay to laugh even when things are dire. Choosing to be miserable isn't lightening anyone else's load."

"We have been doing that, haven't we?" I asked.

"You're getting close to spiraling, sweetie."

I sighed. "Santino and I try to 'stop and smell the flowers.' We try to watch comedies and laugh. We worry we joke too much, that other people will think we're asses, insensitive. Even our friends." I took another bite of the kimchi burger and handed it back to Andy, who took another bite after me.

Santino nodded. "We worry people will think we're not taking fascism seriously. Or climate breakdown. Or whatever else is happening." He stabbed a slice of pickled red onion with his fork.

Andy laughed.

But that wasn't a joke, was it?

"I don't think there's much doubt you guys take everything way *too* seriously. You probably turn more friends away for that, not because you're not serious enough."

It felt like a slap and yet didn't hurt, though I wasn't sure why.

"I suppose you do laugh an awful lot for a dead guy," I admitted. And I supposed that was a large part of what drew us to him. Other than his beard, dick, ass, and ears.

And paunch. Paunches were sexy, too.

"It's all a balance," Andy said, "and no one draws the line at the same spot. Everyone thinks their spot is the only appropriate one. But we're crushed enough as it is without voluntarily taking on more crushiness."

"Is that a word?"

"It's in the Scrabble dictionary."

"I challenge that."

We spent the rest of the meal only telling each other humorous anecdotes from our past. There really were a lot of them, if we allowed ourselves to remember.

After we paid our check, we decided to walk back to Rainier Beach, not quite an hour away. The day was still cool, partly cloudy, but summer was just around the corner. Three hundred people had drowned in Afghanistan this week from heavy rains. There was new flooding in Germany and Belgium. In India—

Nope.

Azaleas and rhododendrons and lilacs and buttercups were still in bloom. Empress trees dazzled us with their purple flowers. A mother pushing a stroller picked a yellow dandelion for her toddler to enjoy.

Life was what it was. We couldn't ignore reality. But we could focus. A little.

Sometimes.

I called Detective Gamroth as we walked along Rainier Avenue, passing a car repair shop, a pot shop, and a tent in front of a boarded up business. "Is it okay if we go back home now, Detective?" I asked. "Do I need to call the fire investigator? Who gives me the all clear?"

Chapter Eighteen: Jake

It felt as if we'd been gone for weeks. Being "home" mattered. I made a note to start volunteering at the non-profit in Pioneer Square Andy had told us about.

Kayleah had been keeping an eye out for us and knocked on our back door only seconds after we returned and handed us a casserole. "I hope everything gets sorted out fast," she said. "If you need any references for contractors, let me know."

"Thank you," I said. "This means a lot." I accepted the casserole with a nod I hoped conveyed my genuine gratitude. "You have a blessed evening."

Was it acceptable to wish someone a blessed evening the same as you'd wish them a blessed day? This shouldn't be a difficult question. There really was a growing divide, and I was part of it. I used to not have any ill feeling toward the American flag, enjoyed seeing it for the most part, as patriotic as the next guy. Now it carried connotations of homophobia, racism, and Islamophobia. Connotations of police brutality and deportations and insurrection.

The U.S. flag had been coopted. And so had Christianity. I avoided even "good" Christians because I was so afraid of running into the many "bad" ones.

There was another knock on the back door. "Dessert?" Santino asked hopefully.

But when he went to answer, Owen was on our doorstep. "What the hell happened?" He pointed toward the front of the house.

We caught him up with the latest as we dug into Kayleah's casserole. Green beans, cream of mushroom soup, and fried onions. You couldn't go wrong with the classics. Owen polished off over half the dish by himself while the rest of us ate the remainder, not exceptionally hungry after lunch.

Of course, as anyone with a paunch knew, eating wasn't always about hunger.

"My day wasn't nearly as exciting," Owen admitted, "but I did learn something fun."

"Yeah?"

"I can swim laps without worrying about who else might be in the lane. I can use any exercise equipment I want. If someone else is exercising in the same space at the same time, we both get a rush of energy." He flexed his right arm. "I'll be able to keep these muscles."

"Sagging spirits" suddenly took on added meaning.

"We might need to hire you at some point to give us advice on how to get in better shape," Santino said. "Recommend a good gym."

"And just how do you plan to pay me?" Owen grinned. "Trading 'services' isn't going to cut it."

"You come up with the terms," I said, taking his comment seriously. "It's only fair."

"Maybe I'll have you pay friends of mine," he replied with a shrug. "Pretend you're taking their advice but you listen to mine."

After dinner, Owen washed dishes while Andy queued up some music. By the time Owen joined us in the living room, Santino had set up the Scrabble board.

"You guys really are nerds," Owen said.

"You say that like it's a good thing," I noted.

"It is."

"Have a seat." Santino motioned to the floor beside the coffee table, where he'd placed a throw pillow. "Tonight, we're only spelling words related to sex," he said. "Slang is allowed. Multiple words, too, if you have enough letters."

"Shouldn't be hard to use the X."

"Or the J."

"Can I coin a new word," Owen asked, "when I need to use a Z?"

"Only if we like the activity you make up the word for."

"You'll have to explain it in detail."

"Maybe act it out in pantomime."

"Can I draw a picture?"

"Only if I can be the model," Andy said.

"For fuck's sake, can we play the damn game already?"

***

The karaoke machine wasn't due to arrive for another week. It was getting a bit late to be making noise anyway. Andy lowered the music. I sat with him on the sofa, Santino sitting on the floor at his feet and Owen sitting before me. Rubbing the back of Owen's head was even more satisfying than rubbing the back of my own.

We stayed up late talking about childhood pets and vacations until Owen announced it was time for him to take off for the evening. "I really do like sleeping at the bathhouse," he said. "If I'm in a public area and someone ends up sitting on me or lying down in the same spot, it sparks a great REM cycle."

Santino, Andy, and I watched an episode of *El don de Alba* after he left, not worrying about the time. There was far too much going on to plan on working the next day. Santino and I would be calling in sick. Andy was the sane one, pulling us to the bedroom sometime after midnight. We cuddled up in bed, fully clothed in case we had to run out again in the middle of the night, and fell asleep within minutes.

***

We should have taken turns keeping watch. We hadn't even thought to ask the detectives if a police cruiser would try to pass by at regular intervals.

[Note to researchers: it's remotely possible that people under long-term stress don't make the most rational decisions.]

A bright light and clap of thunder jolted me awake, and I saw Andy's coworker Wickens standing over the bed, pointing a pistol in our direction. It took less than a second for my brain to return to full alertness.

He must have fired, I realized. I quickly looked at Santino and Andy. They seemed okay.

Could Andy be killed a second time? It had happened in one of the shows we watched.

"You freaks are everywhere," Wickens spat. "You multiply like rats." His lip curled in disgust. "You're an invasive species. We have no choice but to eradicate you."

Part of me wondered how many pathetic metaphors he could come up with. But most of me was terrified.

Wickens didn't smile or laugh maniacally like crazed villains in movies. "It's not just God's will," he said, "which it is. It's self-defense."

"It" was murder.

I couldn't move with Wickens's gun pointed right at me, only inches away. Neither could Santino. "Andy!" I whispered. But there was nothing I could ask of him. I wished Owen were here, too. I looked into Andy's eyes as he stood beside his former coworker, unable to grab the gun. I squeezed Santino's hand underneath the covers.

Wickens shook his head. "I don't *like* using mousetraps," he said. "I don't *like* killing flies." He sighed. "But it has to be done." He adjusted his aim. I'd be killed first. Thank God.

He fired, and I felt a searing pain in my arm.

I tried to push and kick Santino to the edge of the bed, but we were both tangled up in the sheets. Then I tried to scramble to the other side. The man couldn't aim in two directions as the same time.

Wickens fired again. The bullet missed me and there was no time to look for where it had struck. I picked up the first object within reach and flung it toward the man.

He raised his arm to protect himself, the dildo bouncing off his elbow and falling to the floor.

He looked to see what had hit him and then glared at me with more hatred than I thought humanly possible.

Suddenly, Wickens stood up straighter, a puzzled expression on his face. He looked down again, and I could see a huge wet spot forming in his crotch. He was pissing himself. Then slowly, he began turning the gun away from us, toward the wall. Yet his hand kept moving. The man's eyes widened as he realized what was happening. He soon had the barrel of the pistol touching his temple.

"What…?" he huffed. "You…you…!"

"Andy!" Santino shouted.

"You're demons!" Wickens hissed. "You summon devils!"

I stole a glance at Santino, whose face was filled not with terror but anguish. Had he been shot? "Andy," Santino begged, "don't be a killer like him!"

I looked for another weapon. The bedside lamp might kill the guy, too, if I whacked him in the head, but we'd still have a better chance of subduing him alive with that. I tried to grab the lamp, but the cord was still plugged into the wall, and my arm was burning.

I didn't know what I wanted Andy to do. Was it *wrong* to kill a murderer bent on killing even more innocent people? What if we subdued him, called the police, and the justice system failed us as it failed so many others?

Wickens slowly moved the gun away from his head and pointed it at his knee. "Please," the murderer begged.

Then he pointed it at his crotch.

"Oh my God."

"Andy!" Santino shouted.

"Andy can do what he thinks is best," I said calmly, though my heart was racing.

"You…you…you…" Wickens spluttered. Then he shot himself in the foot.

Wickens screamed. So did Andy. They shared every nerve ending.

"Andy!" Santino and I shouted together.

Andy suddenly appeared beside Wickens, who fell to the floor, holding his foot and squealing. Andy's eyes were wide, his hand on his heart. Santino ran around the side of the bed, kicked the gun away, and grabbed his phone. I hurried over to Andy and pulled him into the tightest bear hug ever, getting blood all over him.

Wickens cried.

Epilogue: Andy

Kayleah had called 9-1-1 when she heard the first gunshot, but it still took a few minutes before officers could arrive. The police department was low both in staffing and morale.

While they were on their way, Santino blurted out every word he knew in other languages, making up a few of his own on the spot, and told Wickens he was speaking in tongues. He explained that God was using him as a vessel to condemn Wickens for his sins.

"It was worth a shot," he told me later. "Whether or not God is real, what that creep was basing his life on was superstition."

Santino used the man's most powerful weapon against him.

And I did my part, too.

A forensics team could use Luminol to find traces of blood not visible to the naked eye. Ghosts, it turned out, were also useful for solving crimes. While Wickens couldn't see me—or Owen, who visited him in jail twice—Jake and Santino were able to convince him that it was my ghost who'd possessed him. Together, we threatened that unless he made a complete confession to the police, I'd possess him in jail and force him to offer his ass to every other man awaiting trial as well as to every guard. And once in prison, to every man there. I'd make him beg for it, they told him.

It was unlikely I'd have been able to put any of that into practice, even if I wanted to, but Wickens didn't need to know.

He made a full confession.

I wasn't his first murder. Wickens had started out over a year ago vandalizing property, spray painting homophobic and transphobic slurs on sidewalks, random buildings, and then the cars of people he suspected of "immorality."

He'd then escalated his attacks by mowing down Owen as he rode his bike one morning. Wickens had a pal he knew from church who did bodywork and understood enough of "the mission" to repair all evidence of the collision without reporting him.

Yes, people of any religious background could be creeps, and atheists, too, but *puh-lease*.

Wickens explained that he knew "they" would prevail in November. Lots of wicked people would be killed on Election Day and he wanted to help prepare the way. He drugged me in the restaurant and followed me out a minute later, pulling me into the alley and stabbing me himself. Thank God the Rohypnol kept me from remembering that horror, even as I listened to him tell the detectives.

Detective Gamroth told Jake and Santino she never did suspect them of my murder but knew there were things they weren't telling her. She didn't press, and they didn't offer, and so that was that for now.

Wickens had continued escalating, breaking into Roland's house, spurred by the scene he made in the bank. Wickens zapped him with a stun gun before tying him up. He made Roland watch as he prayed over him and then stabbed him in the heart.

There are some details I wish I didn't know. But I'd demanded a full confession, and Wickens desperately wanted to avoid prison sex.

Good luck with that, buddy.

Wickens had moved up to trying to kill two people next. If he'd succeeded with Jake and Santino, who knew what he might have done next?

Owen popped into the interrogation room with me and thrust himself into the guard leading Wickens away afterward, making the man trip our killer so that he hit his head against the wall.

We never did see Roland's ghost. Perhaps he didn't want to hang out with his ex and his ex's two new lovers. Understandable. Owen appeared to move on after Wickens was sentenced. We figured he'd "walked into the light" or whatever it was one's essence did when it crossed into the realm from which there really was no return.

But every couple of months, he'd show up to play. Not officially part of our committed relationship. Just a ghostly fuck buddy.

Who knew that was a thing?

He did come along when we spent three days camping in the Hoh rainforest.

A week before the election, Jake suggested we celebrate an early Christmas "just in case." Several prominent Republican leaders were still refusing to say they'd accept the results. Santino bought me a pair of bright blue socks with a triceratops head poking out of an egg. Jake gave me a pair of tattoo sleeves with dragons on them. I surprised them both by managing to make a mold of my erect penis and then produce a personalized double-ended dildo for them to share.

"Just in case" they lived and I disappeared.

And now here we are on the eve of the election. There's already been some violence. It's odd to feel scared even after you're dead. But we've made as many contingency plans as we reasonably can. Including a list of "Things to Do When Life Goes On."

We'd ask Owen to act as officiator when I marry Jake and Santino on the anniversary of our first night together.

We'd try to make fossil fuel execs and political stooges piss themselves in public.

We'd limit the news and social media to five minutes in the morning and thirty minutes in the evening.

Jake and Santino would have a date night each week, Jake and I would have a date night each week, Santino and I would have a date night each week, and all three of us would have a date night each week. Date nights could include other friends when applicable. They could include volunteer work or protests. Or reading a book together.

There was a new one out, *Doing It Person Style*, about a shapeshifter who could turn into a dog and act like a pet after a fascist takeover so his human lover could escape detection. And turn back into a man in the bedroom.

Jake and Santino would join a co-op gym in south Seattle and enjoy their physical bodies a bit more.

We'd go to a karaoke bar at least once a month.

And it was always possible I'd start shadowing suspects in other murders and see if I could help wrangle a few more confessions.

The possibilities were endless, all the way to the end. Jake and Santino had both gotten their first tattoos and were deciding what they might like for their second. Jake dyed his hair blue for the first time while Santino dyed his hair purple.

I studied French because it was something I'd always wanted to do.

And I learned cross stitch. Whatever happened, for now every day we'd see the framed quote on the wall I'd worked painstakingly on:

Love each other like there's no tomorrow. And love each other like there is.

Books by Johnny Townsend

Thanks for reading! If you enjoyed this book, could you please take a few minutes to write a review online? Reviews are helpful both to me as an author and to other readers, so we'd all sincerely appreciate your writing one! And if you did enjoy the book, here are some others I've written you might want to look up:

Mormon Underwear

A Gay Mormon Missionary in Pompeii

The Golem of Rabbi Loew

Marginal Mormons

Sexual Solidarity

The Mysterious Madness of Mormons

Going-Out-Of-Religion Sale

Escape from Zion

Gayrabian Nights

Invasion of the Spirit Snatchers

Sins of the Saints

Mormon Misfits

Gay Gaslighting

Out of the Missionary's Closet

A Mormon Motive for Murder

Breaking the Promise of the Promised Land

Mormon Misfits

I Will, Through the Veil

Am I My Planet's Keeper?

Have Your Cum and Eat It, Too

Strangers with Benefits

Constructing Equity

Wake Up and Smell the Missionaries

Racism by Proxy

Orgy at the STD Clinic

Please Evacuate

Recommended Daily Humanity

The Camper Killings

Repent! The End of Capitalism is Nigh!

10 Things to Do Before the Apocalypse

Kinky Quilts: Patchwork Designs for Gay Men

An Eternity of Mirrors: Best Short Stories of Johnny Townsend

Inferno in the French Quarter: The UpStairs Lounge Fire

Latter-Gay Saints: An Anthology of Gay Mormon Fiction (co-editor)

> Available from your favorite online or neighborhood bookstore.

Wondering what some of those other books are about? Read on!

Gayrabian Nights

Gayrabian Nights is a twist on the well-known classic, *1001 Arabian Nights*, in which Scheherazade, under the threat of death if she ceases to captivate King Shahryar's attention, enchants him through a series of mysterious, adventurous, and romantic tales.

In this variation, a male escort, invited to the hotel room of a closeted, homophobic Mormon senator, learns that the man is poised to vote on a piece of anti-gay legislation the following morning. To prevent him from sleeping, so that the exhausted senator will miss casting his vote on the Senate floor, the escort entertains him with stories of homophobia, celibacy, mixed orientation marriages, reparative therapy, coming out, first love, gay marriage, and long-term successful gay relationships.

The escort crafts the stories to give the senator a crash course in gay culture and sensibilities, hoping to bring the man closer to accepting his own sexual orientation.

Inferno in the French Quarter: The UpStairs Lounge Fire

On Gay Pride Day in 1973, someone set the entrance to a French Quarter gay bar on fire. In the terrible inferno that followed, thirty-two people lost their lives, including a third of the local congregation of the Metropolitan Community Church, their pastor burning to death halfway out a second-story window as he tried to claw his way to freedom.

A mother who'd gone to the bar with her two gay sons died alongside them. A man who'd helped his friend escape first was found dead near the fire escape. Two children waited outside a movie theater across town for a father and "uncle" who would never pick them up. During this era of rampant homophobia, several families refused to claim the bodies, and many churches refused to bury the dead.

Author Johnny Townsend pored through old records and tracked down survivors of the fire as well as relatives and friends of those killed to compile this fascinating account of a forgotten moment in gay history.

This second edition on the 50th anniversary of the fire includes additional research and information not available previously.

A Gay Mormon Missionary in Pompeii

What is a gay Mormon missionary doing in Italy? He is trying to save his own soul as well as the souls of others. In these tales chronicling the two-year mission of Robert Anderson, we see a young man tormented by his inability to be the man the Church says he should be. In addition to his personal hell, Anderson faces a major earthquake, organized crime, a serious bus accident, and much more. He copes with horrendous mission leaders and his own suicidal tendencies. But one day, he meets another missionary who loves him, and his world changes forever.

Wake Up and Smell the Missionaries

Two Mormon missionaries in Italy discover they share the same rare ability—both can emit pheromones on demand. At first, they playfully compete in the hills of Frascati to see who can tempt "investigators" most. But soon they're targeting each other non-stop.

Can two immature young men learn to control their "superpower" to live a normal life…and develop genuine love? Even as their relationship is threatened by the attentions of another man?

They seem just on the verge of success when a massive earthquake leaves them trapped under the rubble of their apartment in Castellammare.

With night falling and temperatures dropping, can they dig themselves out in time to save themselves? And will their injuries destroy the ability that brought them together in the first place?

Orgy at the STD Clinic

Todd Tillotson is struggling to move on after his husband is killed in a hit and run attack a year earlier during a Black Lives Matter protest in Seattle.

In this novel set entirely on public transportation, we watch as Todd, isolated throughout the pandemic, battles desperation in his attempt to safely reconnect with the world.

Will he find love again, even casual friendship, or will he simply end up another crazy old man on the bus?

Things don't look good until a man whose face he can't even see sits down beside him despite the raging variants.

And asks him a question that will change his life.

Please Evacuate

A gay, partygoing New Yorker unconcerned about the future or the unsustainability of capitalism is hit by a truck and thrust into a straight man's body half a continent away. As Hunter tries to figure out what's happening, he's caught up in another disaster, a wildfire sweeping through a Colorado community, the flames overtaking him and several schoolchildren as they flee.

When he awakens, Hunter finds himself in the body of yet another man, this time in northern Italy, a former missionary about to marry a young Mormon woman. Still piecing together this new reality, and beginning to embrace his latest identity, Hunter fights for his life in a devastating flash flood along with his wife *and* his new husband.

He's an aging worker in drought-stricken Texas, a nurse at an assisted living facility in the direct path of a hurricane, an advocate for the unhoused during a freak Seattle blizzard.

We watch as Hunter is plunged into life after life, finally recognizing the futility of only looking out for #1 and understanding the part he must play in addressing the global climate crisis…if he ever gets another chance.

The Camper Killings

When a homeless man is found murdered a few blocks from Morgan Beylerian's house in south Seattle, everyone seems to consider the body just so much additional trash to be cleared from the neighborhood. But Morgan liked the guy. They used to chat when Morgan brought Nick groceries once a week.

And the brutal way the man was killed reminds Morgan of their shared Mormon heritage, back when the faithful agreed to have their throats slit if they ever revealed temple secrets.

Did Nick's former wife take action when her ex-husband refused to grant a temple divorce? Did his murder have something to do with the public accusations that brought an end to his promising career?

Morgan does his best to investigate when no one else seems to care, but it isn't easy as a man living paycheck to paycheck himself, only able to pursue his investigation via public transit.

As he continues his search for the killer, Morgan's friends withdraw and his husband threatens to leave. When another homeless man is killed and Morgan is accused of the crime, things look even bleaker.

But his troubles aren't over yet.

Will Morgan find the killer before the killer finds him?

Kinky Quilts

Since patchwork quilts are usually displayed in bedrooms where couples engage in sex, why are there so few quilt designs for folks who want a bit of sexual energy in these intimate spaces?

The original designs in this volume range from simple to intermediate, and with over 250 to choose from, even beginner quilters will find patterns tempting enough to get started.

In *Kinky Quilts*, Johnny Townsend has collected his best designs from *Quilting Beyond the Rainbow*, *Gay Sleeping Arrangements*, and *Queer Quilting*, to offer fun, sexy quilts for men who love men.

What Readers Have Said

Townsend's stories are "a gay *Portnoy's Complaint* of Mormonism. Salacious, sweet, sad, insightful, insulting, religiously ethnic, quirky-faithful, and funny."

D. Michael Quinn, author of *The Mormon Hierarchy: Origins of Power*

"Told from a believably conversational first-person perspective, [*A Gay Mormon Missionary in Pompeii*'s] novelistic focus on Anderson's journey to thoughtful self-acceptance allows for greater character development than often seen in short stories, which makes this well-paced work rich and satisfying, and one of Townsend's strongest. An extremely important contribution to the field of Mormon fiction." Named to Kirkus Reviews' Best of 2011.

Kirkus Reviews

"The thirteen stories in *Mormon Underwear* capture this struggle [between Mormonism and homosexuality] with humor, sadness, insight, and sometimes shocking details....*Mormon Underwear* provides compelling stories, literally from the inside-out."

Niki D'Andrea, *Phoenix New Times*

"Townsend's lively writing style and engaging characters [in *Zombies for Jesus*] make for stories which force us to wake up, smell the (prohibited) coffee, and review our attitudes with regard to reading dogma so doggedly. These are tales which revel in the individual tics and quirks which make us human, Mormon or not, gay or not…"

A.J. Kirby, *The Short Review*

"The Rift," from *A Gay Mormon Missionary in Pompeii*, is a "fascinating tale of an untenable situation…a *tour de force*."

David Lenson, editor, *The Massachusetts Review*

"Pronouncing the Apostrophe," from *The Golem of Rabbi Loew*, is "quiet and revealing, an intriguing tale…"

Sima Rabinowitz, Literary Magazine Review, *NewPages.com*

The Circumcision of God is "a collection of short stories that consider the imperfect, silenced majority of Mormons, who may in fact be [the Church's] best hope.…[The book leaves] readers regretting the church's willingness to marginalize those who best exemplify its ideals: those who love fiercely despite all obstacles, who brave challenges at great personal risk and who always choose the hard, higher road."

Kirkus Reviews

In *Mormon Fairy Tales*, Johnny Townsend displays "both a wicked sense of irony and a deep well of compassion."

Kel Munger, *Sacramento News and Review*

Zombies for Jesus is "eerie, erotic, and magical."

Publishers Weekly

"While [Townsend's] many touching vignettes draw deeply from Mormon mythology, history, spirituality and culture, [*Mormon Fairy Tales*] is neither a gaudy act of proselytism nor angry protest literature from an ex-believer. Like all good fiction, his stories are simply about the joys, the hopes and the sorrows of people."

Kirkus Reviews

"In *Inferno in the French Quarter* author Johnny Townsend restores this tragic event [the UpStairs Lounge fire] to its proper place in LGBT history and reminds us that the victims of the blaze were not just 'statistics,' but real people with real lives, families, and friends."

Jesse Monteagudo, *The Bilerico Project*

In *Inferno in the French Quarter*, "Townsend's heart-rending descriptions of the victims...seem to [make them] come alive once more."

Kit Van Cleave, *OutSmart Magazine*

"While [*Inferno in the French Quarter*] is a non-fiction work, the author is a skilled fiction [writer], so he manages to respect the realism of the story, while at the same time recreating their lives and voices. It's probably thanks to the [author's] skills that this piece of non-fiction goes well beyond a simple recording of events."

Elisa Rolle, *Rainbow Awards*

Marginal Mormons is "an irreverent, honest look at life outside the mainstream Mormon Church....Throughout his musings on sin and forgiveness, Townsend beautifully demonstrates his characters' internal, perhaps irreconcilable struggles....Rather than anger and disdain, he offers an honest portrayal of people searching for meaning and community in their lives, regardless of their life choices or secrets." Named to Kirkus Reviews' Best of 2012.

Kirkus Reviews

The stories in *The Mormon Victorian Society* "register the new openness and confidence of gay life in the age of same-sex marriage....What hasn't changed is Townsend's wry, conversational prose, his subtle evocations of character and social dynamics, and his deadpan humor. His warm empathy still glows in this intimate yet clear-eyed engagement with Mormon theology and folkways. Funny, shrewd and finely wrought dissections of the awkward contradictions—and surprising harmonies—between conscience and desire." Named to Kirkus Reviews' Best of 2013.

Kirkus Reviews

"This collection of short stories [*The Mormon Victorian Society*] featuring gay Mormon characters slammed [me] in the face from the first page, wrestled my heart and mind to the floor, and left me panting and wanting more by the end. Johnny Townsend has created so many memorable characters in such few pages. I went weeks thinking about this book. It truly touched me."

Tom Webb, *A Bear on Books*

Dragons of the Book of Mormon is an "entertaining collection....Townsend's prose is sharp, clear, and easy to read, and his characters are well rendered..."

Publishers Weekly

"The pre-eminent documenter of alternative Mormon lifestyles...Townsend has a deep understanding of his characters, and his limpid prose, dry humor and well-grounded (occasionally magical) realism make their spiritual conundrums both compelling and entertaining. [*Dragons of the Book of Mormon* is] [a]nother of Townsend's critical but affectionate and absorbing tours of Mormon discontent." Named to Kirkus Reviews' Best of 2014.

Kirkus Reviews

In *Gayrabian Nights*, "Townsend's prose is always limpid and evocative, and…he finds real drama and emotional depth in the most ordinary of lives."

Kirkus Reviews

Gayrabian Nights is a "complex revelation of how seriously soul damaging the denial of the true self can be."

Ryan Rhodes, author of *Free Electricity*

Gayrabian Nights "was easily the most original book I've read all year. Funny, touching, topical, and thoroughly enjoyable."

Rainbow Awards

Lying for the Lord is "one of the most gripping books that I've picked up for quite a while. I love the author's writing style, alternately cynical, humorous, biting, scathing, poignant, and touching…. This is the third book of his that I've read, and all are equally engaging. These are stories that need to be told, and the author does it in just the right way."

    Heidi Alsop, *Ex-Mormon Foundation Board Member*

In *Lying for the Lord*, Townsend "gets under the skin of his characters to reveal their complexity and conflicts....shrewd, evocative [and] wryly humorous."

Kirkus Reviews

In *Missionaries Make the Best Companions*, "the author treats the clash between religious dogma and liberal humanism with vivid realism, sly humor, and subtle feeling as his characters try to figure out their true missions in life. Another of Townsend's rich dissections of Mormon failures and uncertainties..." Named to Kirkus Reviews' Best of 2015.

Kirkus Reviews

In *Invasion of the Spirit Snatchers*, "Townsend, a confident and practiced storyteller, skewers the hypocrisies and eccentricities of his characters with precision and affection. The outlandish framing narrative is the most consistent source of shock and humor, but the stories do much to ground the reader in the world—or former world—of the characters....A funny, charming tale about a group of Mormons facing the end of the world."

Kirkus Reviews

"Townsend's collection [*The Washing of Brains*] once again displays his limpid, naturalistic prose, skillful narrative chops, and his subtle insights into psychology...Well-crafted dispatches on the clash between religion and self-fulfillment..."

Kirkus Reviews

"While the author is generally at his best when working as a satirist, there are some fine, understated touches in these tales [*The Last Days Linger*] that will likely affect readers in subtle ways....readers should come away impressed by the deep empathy he shows for all his characters—even the homophobic ones."

Kirkus Reviews

"Written in a conversational style that often uses stories and personal anecdotes to reveal larger truths, this immensely approachable book [*Racism by Proxy*] skillfully serves its intended audience of White readers grappling with complex questions regarding race, history, and identity. The author's frequent references to the Church of Jesus Christ of Latter-day Saints may be too niche for readers unfamiliar with its idiosyncrasies, but Townsend generally strikes a perfect balance of humor, introspection, and reasoned arguments that will engage even skeptical readers."

Kirkus Reviews

Orgy at the STD Clinic portrays "an all-too real scenario that Townsend skewers to wincingly accurate proportions…[with] instant classic moments courtesy of his punchy, sassy, sexy lead character…"

Jim Piechota, *Bay Area Reporter*

Orgy at the STD Clinic is "…a triumph of humane sensibility. A richly textured saga that brilliantly captures the fraying social fabric of contemporary life." Named to Kirkus Reviews' Best Indie Books of 2022.

Kirkus Reviews

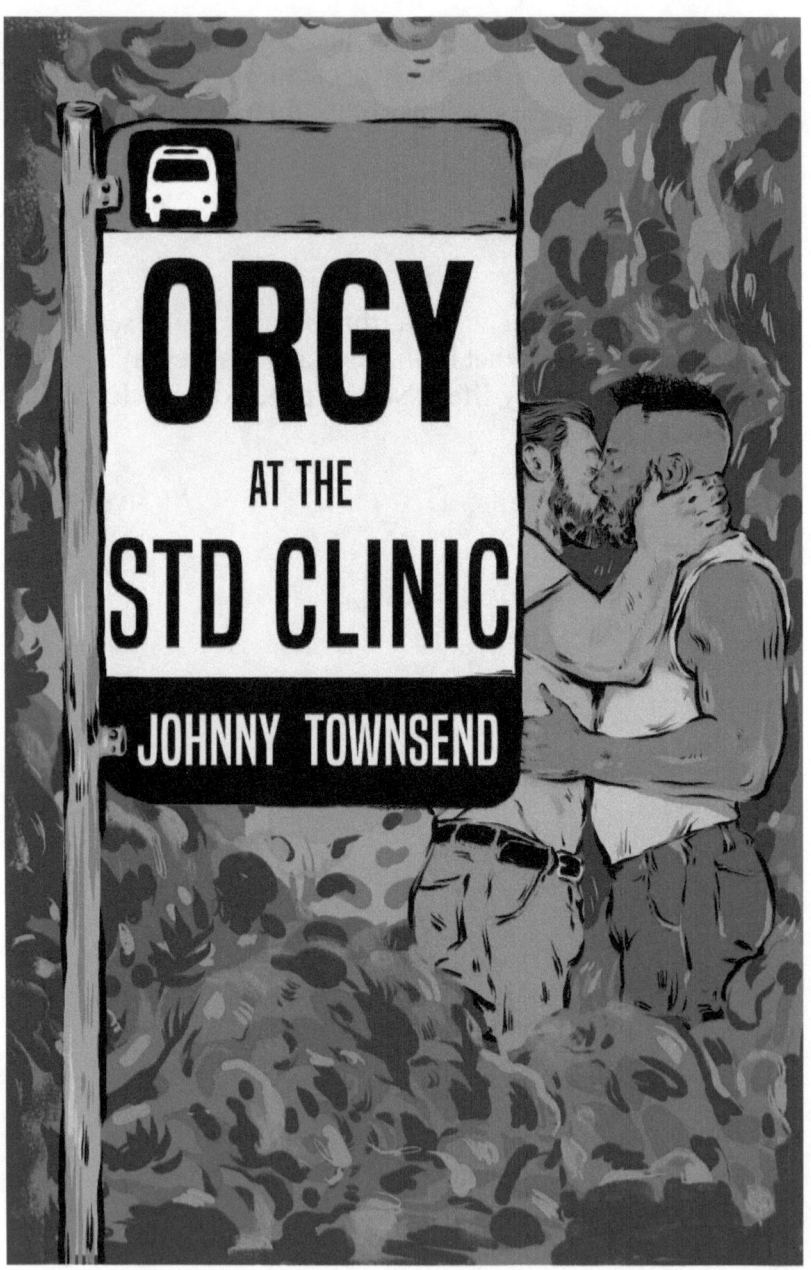

10 Things to Do Before the Apocalypse

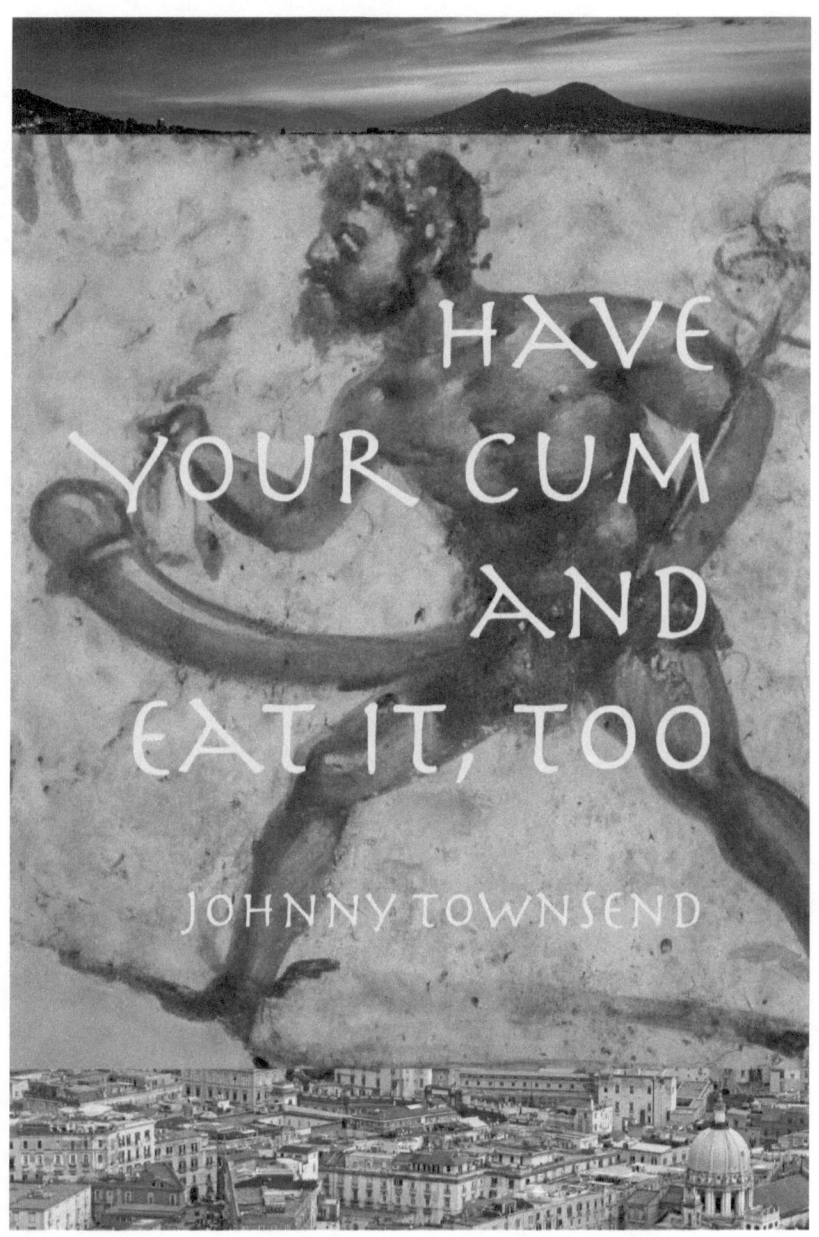

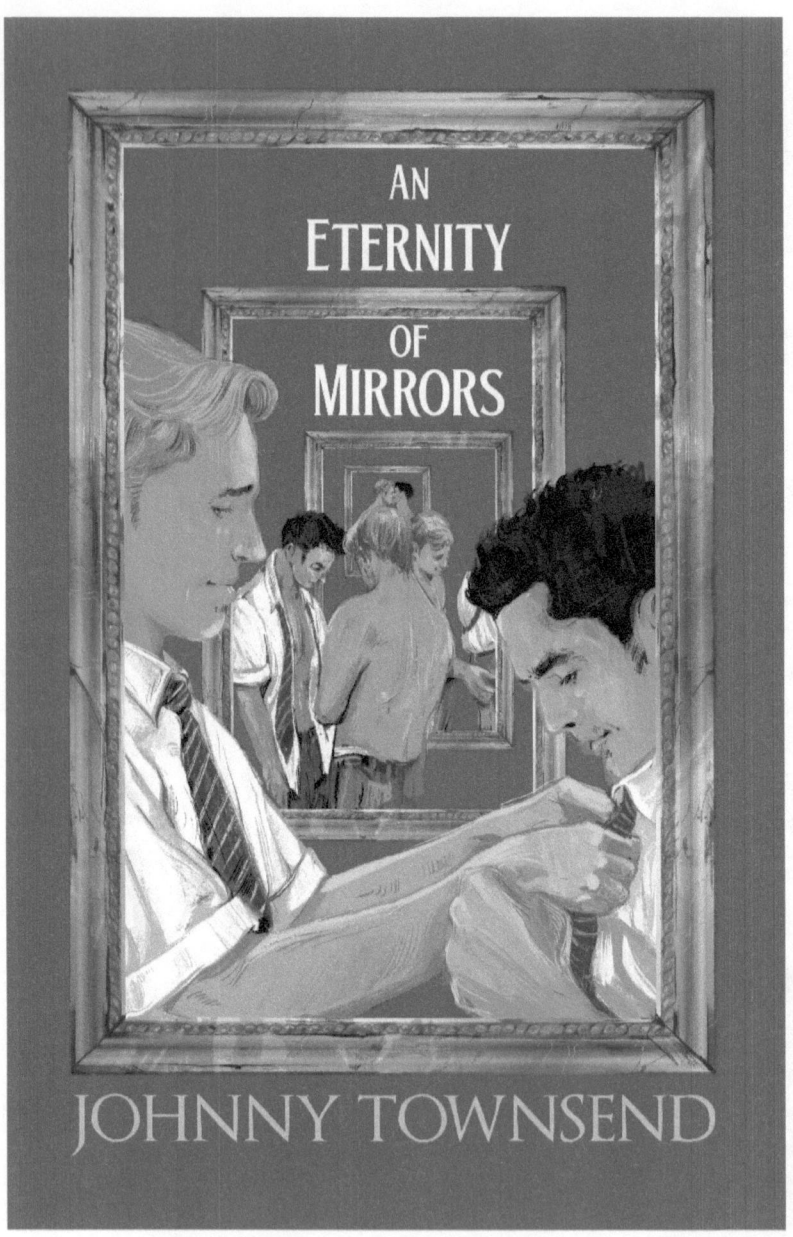

10 Things to Do Before the Apocalypse

www.ingramcontent.com/pod-product-compliance
Lightning Source LLC
LaVergne TN
LVHW040050080526
838202LV00045B/3569